Contemporary
Mexican-American
Women Novelists

Wor(l)ds of Change
Latin American and Iberian Literature

Kathleen March
General Editor

Vol. 3

PETER LANG
New York • Washington, D.C./Baltimore
Bern • Frankfurt am Main • Berlin • Vienna • Paris

María C. González

Contemporary
Mexican-American
Women Novelists

Toward a Feminist Identity

PETER LANG
New York • Washington, D.C./Baltimore
Bern • Frankfurt am Main • Berlin • Vienna • Paris

Library of Congress Cataloging-in-Publication Data

González, María C.
Contemporary Mexican-American women novelists: toward
a feminist identity / María C. González.
p. cm. — (Wor(l)ds of change; vol. 3)
Includes bibliographical references and index.
1. American fiction—Mexican American authors—History and criticism.
2. Feminism and literature—United States—History—20th century. 3. Women
and literature—United States—History—20th century. 4. Mexican American
women—Intellectual life—20th century. 5. American fiction—Women
authors—History and criticism. 6. American fiction—20th century—History
and criticism. 7. Mexican American women in literature. 8. Mexican
Americans in literature. I. Title. II. Series.
PS153.M4G66   813'.54099287—dc20   93-50801
ISBN 0-8204-2415-3
ISSN 1072-334X

Die Deutsche Bibliothek-CIP-Einheitsaufnahme

González, María C.:
Contemporary Mexican-American women novelists: toward a feminist
identity / María C. González. –New York; Washington, D.C./Baltimore;
Bern; Frankfurt am Main; Berlin; Vienna; Paris: Lang.
(Wor(l)ds of change; Vol. 3)
ISBN 0-8204-2415-3
NE: GT

The paper in this book meets the guidelines for permanence and durability
of the Committee on Production Guidelines for Book Longevity
of the Council of Library Resources.

Printed in the United States of America.

Dedication

To my parents, Carmen A. González and Luis N. González,
who have always believed
in the work I do.

Acknowledgments

This work is the product of many individuals who have given unselfishly of their time and education. First, I must thank and acknowledge my computer guru and good friend, Wesley W. Fryar. His willingness to put in time and hard work for no compensation and less fun is greatly appreciated. May you find great satisfaction in this book.

Dr. Marlene Longenecker first began this saga with me, and her continued wisdom has never waivered. I would also like to thank Dr. Keith Walters, Dr. James Battersby, Dr. Patrick Mullen, and the late Dr. Josaphat Kubayanda for providing much of the initial direction in developing this text. I must also acknowledge Dr. Connie S. Ringger for having been once a part of my life and this project.

The editing skills of Dr. MaryJo Wagner have always made my work stronger. The final proofing and indexing assistance by Merlyn Pulikkathara was most valuable.

As ever, I thank my family. My brothers, Louie, Hector, and Fred, who have provided me with happiness and sisters, Nena, Martha, and Irma; and children to love, Valerie, Louie, Jessica, Joseph, and Jennifer; and my parents, Luis and Carmen, who are the truest gift of all.

This is a text that represents all their best work as well as thoughts. And if the text is of any value, it is because these people were a part of its production.

From *Borderlands/La Frontera: The New Mestiza* (c) 1987 by Gloria Anzaldúa. Reprinted with permission from the publisher, San Francisco: Aunt Lute Books.
From *Trini* by Estella Portillo Trambley. Reprinted with permission from the publisher, Tempe, AZ: Bilingual Press, 1986.
From *Across the Great River* by Irene Beltrán Hernández. Reprinted with permission from the publisher, Houston: Arte Público Press-University of Houston, 1989.

Contents

Introduction

Cherríe Moraga called for a Chicana feminist theory in her book *Loving in the War Years* (1983), a collection of poems and essays.[1] In her essay "A Long Line of Vendidas," she begins her discussion of such a theory and its parallels with African-American feminism: "Contrary to popular belief among Chicanos, Chicana Feminism did not borrow from white feminists to create a movement. If any direct 'borrowing' was done, it was from Black feminists" (132).[2] Moraga claims that the manifesto of the Combahee River Collective in 1977 "had considerable impact in creating an analysis of U.S. Third World women's oppression" (133).[3] For Moraga, the work of African-American feminists represented the beginnings of a feminism relevant to Chicanas:

> When I first discovered it [the Black Feminist Statement] in 1978, there were three things that struck me the most profoundly: one was the lesbian visibility of its authors; second was their expressed solidarity with other women of color; and third was a concern for what might be considered the *psychosexual* oppression of women of color. (133)

Significant to Moraga for the development of a Chicana feminism was the recognition that oppressions take many forms and gender alone could not be the core of a feminist theory for women of color. Thus African-American feminists provided Moraga a framework for an analysis of the interrelations of race, class, and sexual orientation in her expressions of a Chicana feminism. For Moraga, African-American feminists issued the invitation to the expression of a feminism that could account for the matrix of oppressions that included issues significant to a Chicana. This invitation led Moraga to her articulation of Chicana feminism:

> *The right to passion* expressed in our own cultural tongue and
> movements is what this essay ["A Long Line of Vendidas"] seems, finally, to
> be about. I would not be trying to develop some kind of Chicana feminist
> theory if I did not have strong convictions, urgent hunches, and deep racial
> memory that the Chicana could *not* betray a sister, a daughter, a compañera
> in the service of the man and his institutions if somewhere in the chain of
> historical events and generations, she were allowed to love herself as both
> female and mestiza. (136)

This self-love and love for other women represent for Moraga the
basis for a Chicana feminist theory. "When we name this bond
between the women of our race, from this Chicana feminism emerges"
(139). The inability to love oneself because one is female and mestiza
represents the beginning of Chicana feminism's analysis of
oppression.

I. La Malinche

In the introduction to selections from Chicana writings in Dexter
Fisher's *The Third Women* (1980), Mexican folkore helps to explain
the self-hatred Moraga sees in Chicanas:

> In contrast to Guadalupe [the Virgin Mary] and Tonantzin [an Aztec fertility
> goddess], who are mother images of consolation and nourishment, is *La
> Malinche*, "the violated mother." The Indian consort of Cortés and mother
> of his illegitimate children, *La Malinche* (Doña Marina) is said to symbolize
> the Spanish conquest. Her rape opened the way physically and spiritually to
> the defeat of the Indians and the birth of the Mestizo race. (310)[4]

Mexicans trace their ancestry to this rape. Marcela Christine Lucero-
Trujillo in her essay, "The Dilemma of the Modern Chicana Artist and
Critic" (1977), argues that the Chicano movement coupled with a
feminist perspective gave rise to Chicana writings that attempt to
rediscover and retell the story of La Malinche.[5] "The fact that some
Chicanas view Doña Marina in a sympathetic manner in contrast to
the portrayal of Mexican authors may mean that her redefinition may
be a Chicana phenomenon" (326). The redefinition of La Malinche
is, indeed, "a Chicana phenomenon." Norma Alarcón's essay,
"Chicana's Feminist Literature: A Re-Vision Through Malintzin/or
Malintzin: Putting Flesh Back on the Object" (1981), traces La
Malinche images and representations in the poetry of contemporary
Chicana feminist writers.[6] Alarcón, too, claims that Chicana feminist

poets seek to re-address the issue of betrayal and, in their work, to reconceptualize the male myth of La Malinche, Alarcón lists the issues Chicana feminists address as indigenous to themselves:

> The mythic aspects of disavowal, and the historical ambiance of Malintzin merge in Chicana's literature to bring out the following sexual politics theme: 1)to choose among extant patriarchies is not a choice at all; 2) woman's abandonment and orphanhood and psychic/emotional starvation occur even in the midst of tangible family; 3) woman is slave, emotionally as well as economically; 4) women are seen not just by one patriarchy but by all as rapeable and sexually exploitable; 5) blind devotion is not a feasible human choice (this is further clarified by the telling absence of poems by women to the Virgin of Guadalupe, while poems by men to her are plentiful); 6) when there is love/devotion it is at best deeply ambivalent . . . . (187)

Elizabeth J. Ordóñez in "The Concept of Cultural Identity in Chicana Poetry" (1984) also explores the theme of La Malinche and its impact upon the works of Chicana poets: "One of the main aspects of the Chicana's past which cried out for redefinition was the figure and function of La Malinche" (75).

As Moraga argued initially, self-love can only begin the process of creating an indigenous feminism for Chicanas, and this self-love cannot begin without dealing with the cultural trauma of being children of the raped one. Thus re-vision of La Malinche and a preoccupation with what her cultural status has meant for Mexican and Mexican-American women are central to the emergence of Chicana feminism.

II. Feminism and Mexican Americans

Margarita Melville's work *Twice a Minority: Mexican American Women* (1980) explores the concept that Mexican-American women are doubly oppressed, racially by the dominant society in the United States and sexually by rigid gender roles in the Mexican culture. In one of the first articles to discuss Chicanas and the United States women's movement, Marta Cotera argues in "Feminism: The Chicana and Anglo Version: A Historical Analysis" that Mexican-American women have been discriminated against in the white women's movement (227). Melville and Cotera both claim that the white feminist movement is alienating to Chicanas, and this sense of alienation and distrust of white feminism represents a common theme in the writings of Mexican Americans, requiring Chicana writers to explore women's issues on their own terms.[7] The most commonly cited reason for Chicana ambivalence toward Anglo feminism is the fear that it detracts from the concept of *familia* as Tey Diana Rebolledo states in her essay "Walking the Thin Line":

> For the Chicana there is also particular emphasis on family orientation and solidarity.
>
> The Chicana *writer*, however, is an anomaly by definition. She is generally educated and professional with aspirations for self-definition on her own terms. To write is to take control, to express your environment, and to break away from acceptance. The pressures on the Chicana writer to adhere to Raza values involve, among other things, not being a feminist. Feminism has been seen in some senses as opposition to traditonal values and as "acculturation," selling out to Anglo culture. (Rebolledo 94-95).

As this statement implies, the Chicana writer fears becoming La Malinche. One can thus understand why Mexican-American women writers are preoccupied with the redefinition of La Malinche. These writers are attempting to redefine themselves beyond the Mexican community's parameters, without having to accept the burden of being perceived as traitors to or betrayers of their culture.

This question of the Chicana acceptance of a feminist label continues, even though many Chicana writers deal with feminist issues. Eliana Ortega and Nancy Saporta Sternback in "At the Threshold of the Unnamed: Latina Literary Discourse in the Eighties" (1989) make the following observation: "We postulate that even those Latinas who eschew the term feminist are, to some degree, affected by its significance on both theoretical and practical levels" (11).

Beyond Stereotypes: The Critical Analysis of Chicana Literature, published in 1985, was the first book dedicated to the critical analysis of Chicana literature. Edited by María Herrera-Sobek, this volume began filling the vacuum of critical work on Chicana literature. Herrera-Sobek, in her introduction, provides a concise overview of the historical Mexican woman and refutes the stereotypes that have surrounded her. Demanding a reevaluation of Chicanas in the United States, Herrera-Sobek challenges Chicanas:

> Stereotypes need to be broken down. To this end the Chicana is taking the lead. Much, however, still needs to be done to improve the image of these women if we are to provide viable role models for future generations. . . . For it is the Chicana herself, above anyone else, who can explore the intricacies of her womanhood, her intimate self, and her soul and provide the world with a true image of who she is. (24)

This call for self-disclosure defines the objective of this collection, which includes one of the first articles that concentrates exclusively on the study of Chicana novels, "Chicana Novelists in the Process of Creating Fictive Voices" by Francisco Lomelí. Written in the early 1980s, Lomelí claims that the poets have faired far better in terms of critical recognition than the novelists.

> Thus far, Chicana poets have enjoyed some critical discussion, although they have not attained the same attention as their male counter-parts. And, within this panorama of relative neglect toward Chicana creativity in general, the novelists have fared even worse as is evidenced by the alarmingly low number of critical studies devoted to novels written by Chicanas. True, this is partly attributable to the small number of female novelists, a total of four contemporary writers by the early 1980s: Berta Ornelas, *Come Down From the Mound* (1975); Isabella Ríos, *Victuum* (1976); Gina Valdés, *Maria Portillo* (1981); and Estela Portillo Trambley, *Trini*. (30)

With the exception of *Trini*, the novels Lomelí cites are now all out of print. Lomelí's own in-depth discussion of them focuses only on the novels by Ornelas and Ríos. He also lists the number of bibliographical entries available at that time on the works:

> The list may be summarized as follows: one review on Berta Ornelas' novel, one review and one article on Isabella Ríos' work, one interview on Estela Portillo Trambley with no in-depth studies on her forthcoming novel (this does not include the various articles on her dramatic pieces), and one brief critical assessment of Gina Valdés' writing. (46)

This leads Lomelí to conclude that "when Chicana works do appear they are rarely viewed critically. . . .," and "[t]he underlying implication is that the issues women writers raise are not of great magnitude or importance" (32). Lomelí's article "attempts to remedy the obvious oversight on the part of Chicano criticism . . ." (32).

The later 1980s did see a growth of literature and criticism by

and about Mexican-American women writers. Most of the collections
are anthologies of poetry, prose, and some criticism. Books of
poetry have seen the most growth, and novels by Mexican-American
women are being published more consistently. A few presses
represent the bulk of publication houses that regularly publish
Mexican-American women: Arte Público Press of Houston; the
Bilingual Press, originally in Binghamton, New York and now at
Arizona State University in Tempe; and the small women's presses
including Aunt Lute and Third Woman. Journals of course continue
to provide the most up to date research on these authors. *Third
Woman*, *The Americas Review* (originally, *Revista Chicano-Riqueña*),
and *MELUS: Journal of the Society for the Study of Multi-Ethnic
Literature of the United States* regularly publish essays on Chicana
literature.

The contemporary novels I have chosen to study are only a
small representation of the novels now available. I have concentrated
on the first novel for most of the authors who have since published
second and third novels. It is clear that this study does not attempt
to be inclusive of all Mexican-American women novelists now in
print, but it is a beginning. My hope is that this is the first of many
major projects that will take up the issue of contemporary Mexican-
American women novelists.

III. The Novels

In studying the works of Mexican-American women novelists,
I also hope to introduce my readers to novels that in most cases still
remain outside the recognized canon. Since those who read this
discussion may not be familiar with the works I consider and part of
my goal is to familiarize new audiences to Mexican-American
literature, I offer a brief introduction to each novel and writer.

Trini (1986) by Estela Portillo Trambley is a work caught up
with the magic of the old indigenous world of Mexico and the form
it takes in the United States. Written in the third person, the novel is
the story of Trini, a member of the Tarahumara tribe, whose life we
follow from her early childhood in Mexico to her legal residence in
the U. S. at the age of thirty. Interwoven in the narrative is the magic
of the old ways of the Tarahumara tribe as represented by three
dwarfs who interact with Trini throughout her life. As a child, Trini's

playmate is a silent dwarf called El Enano [the dwarf], who is a part of the mysticism of the green and lush valley where Trini's people have lived for centuries. He plays with the children, teaching them how to communicate without words and games that actually represent the ancient culture.

The novel begins with the death of Trini's mother in childbirth, the first of many griefs Trini will suffer throughout her life. When Trini's aunt comes to live with them after the death of Trini's mother, she brings the first intrusion to Trini's idyllic life, an alien Catholicism. Some years later, Trini's father must move the family to a mining town in order to find work, and Trini leaves the simplicity of the valley. Raped by a pimp and left pregnant at fifteen, Trini now confronts the social system that allows men to mistreat her and one that provides no avenue for justice. Although her family is understanding when Trini's child dies at birth, she realizes she must be on her own in order to grow and become a woman. She leaves her family and goes to Chihuahua, a large city where she sells vegetables in the market; here she falls in love with her lover, Tonio, and is again abandoned when Tonio, now her husband, runs away. Trini now moves to Juarez, a Mexican city across the border from El Paso, Texas.

Losing hope and struggling to survive, Trini meets a second silent dwarf. This dwarf, Manuk, is a friend of a retired madam who offers Trini assistance and support. The encounter brings a renewal of self to Trini, who crosses the border to deliver a second child by Sabochi, an old friend and lover. By having the child in the U.S., Trini secures legal status for herself and a chance to make a living for her children. In search of land to buy, Trini once again comes across a dwarf, known as the hermit Salvador [savior]. In exchange for Trini's agreement to stay and befriend him before his impending death, Salvador leaves her his land. At his request, she burns his body and lets the wind scatter his ashes, an act that symbolizes the end of a way of life, the connection with the old tribal rituals. The land is now Trini's, and she brings her family together: her father, her aunt, her wayward husband, Tonio, and the children they continue to have together. The years go by, and Trini's loneliness and continued emotional distancing from her wandering husband who drops in now and then begin to overwhelm her. She realizes the dream of the land is not enough for now she needs a new dream. She finds it in her decision to talk to Rico about his true father, Sabochi, and take him to meet his father.

This novel is rich with the evocations of harsh lives mixed with the mysticism of the old indigenous ways. Portillo Trambley attempts to personalize the migrant history of most Mexican-Americans, the disappearance of the indigenous traditions, and the transformation that occurs once the border is crossed. It is a story of progression, how one society supplants another, most often violently. It is, among other things, a novel which describes cultural displacement, the transformation of Trini from the indigenous Tarahumara child to Mexican to illegal alien to a humble, small landowner, legal alien in the United States. Each painful transformation represents the parallel story of Mexican-American culture. In the end, ownership of land is not enough; dreams of some kind must always exist in order to sustain the mundane. Trini's survival has always depended upon her willingness to work towards a goal. In introducing her son to his indigenous heritage, Trini finds a new goal.

Portillo Trambley, a native El Pasoan novelist and playwright, has written a larger story than just the life of one woman. It is symbolically the story of all Mexican-Americans. Born in 1936, Portillo Trambley has also produced and written dramas including *Sor Juana and Other Plays* (1983).

Delia's Song (1989) by Lucha Corpi concerns the development of a young writer. The story begins with Delia going to a costume party to celebrate the completion of her Ph.D. at the University of California at Berkeley. Through stream-of-consciousness techniques and flashbacks, Corpi begins with Delia as a shy, serious girl, a freshman at Berkeley, unprepared for 1968 and the turbulence of the student uprisings and campus turmoil which eventually lead to violent confrontations between students and police authorities. Recording the activities and interactions of MASC (Mexican-American Student Confederation), later called MECHA (Movimiento Estudiantil Chicano de Aztlán), Delia begins her chronicle of the Berkeley campus from a Chicana point of view.

The novel describes the development of Delia from "Mexican-American" to politicized Chicana, from an innocent freshman to battle weary student activist, from a naive young lady to a worldly woman. She discovers that the price for student activism in 1969 is high. The group of students she joins as a member of MASC leave school, transfer to other campuses, or drop out of society. Completing the Ph.D. leaves Delia emotionally exhausted. She is haunted by the ghosts of Berkeley's activist days and the past deaths of her brothers, one a junkie, the other a Vietnam statistic. The novel returns to the costume party where Delia meets someone dressed as James Joyce. The second half of the novel focuses on her attempt to make sense of her past through writing. She has an affair with the man dressed as James Joyce, whose name is Roger Hart, but when her long lost love, Jeff Morónes, from the activist days returns, it becomes clear to Delia that it is he whom she loves.

Told in the third person, except in the stream-of-consciousness sections, the story of Delia is the story of a woman coming to know herself as a writer, finding her own voice. This rather unsuccessful novel is semi-autobiographical, a fictionalization of the author's own turbulent student days. Corpi's books include collections of poems *Palabras de mediodía/Noon Words* (1980), *Variaciones sobre una tempestad/Variations On a Storm* (1990), and another novel, the prize winning, *Eulogy for a Brown Buffalo* (1992).

Maravilla (1989), Laura del Fuego's first novel, is a first-person narrative told by Consuelo "Cece" Contreres, an East Los Angeles barrio girl. Raised on street language, Cece is a girl of her times though she hears Teresa de Avila's voice with a Mexican accent and speaks to her three times, each time when she is in serious trouble. Despite her mystical connection to St. Teresa, Cece leads the typical life of the barrio girl in the early sixties: joins a girl's club, the Belltones; gets into trouble at school; drinks; wears lots of makeup; and cruises the streets of Los Angeles. Cece meets Gerry Rodriguez and discovers a friendship closer than sisterhood. Sharing the adventures of having boyfriends, going to parties, and being teenagers on the streets, Gerry and Cece live ordinary lives until a friend gets shot in the back by a cop while Cece stands watching. She becomes depressed, gets sick, and is put into the hospital where she is comforted by a second vision of St. Teresa.

The streets of Los Angeles offer Cece and her friends drugs, death, and eternal "project" dwellings. Cece and Gerry end up with boyfriends who are junkies. Cece's boyfriend dies after being set-up by Gerry's boyfriend. Cece is left pregnant and in search of an abortion. The stark details of an illegal abortion are unrepresented in the narrative, for Cece loses consciousness during the operation.

Gerry finds herself in a miserable marriage. Cece attempts to write but is unable to combat the depression which blocks her writing. One night, Cece dreams she sees St. Teresa sitting at a desk writing. On a sheet of paper, St. Teresa has written "RITE." Cece wakes up and finally begins to write. Gerry calls from San Francisco, where she is living, to get Cece's help in getting out of her marriage. Cece then rescues Gerry who asks her to move in. Cece decides it is time to leave the barrio, with all its ghosts, behind. Marcos, Gerry's brother, has recently returned from Vietnam and, like Gerry and Cece, is in need of healing. The three move into an apartment together. The war-ravaged survivors are going to attempt to heal each other and themselves, each in her or his own way. Thus, the novels ends with the hope that the characters will find peace with each other.

   The Wedding (1989) by Mary Helen Ponce is a hilarious novel set in a barrio near Los Angeles in the nineteen fifties. As the title indicates, the novel focuses on the wedding of Blanca Munoz and Sammy, known as Cricket, a neighborhood gang leader. The tale of how Blanca meets Cricket, falls in love, agrees to marry him, and prepares for the wedding comprises the story. The novel includes colorful characters: Cricket's sidekick, Tudi, a scared-of-his-shadow-follower, and Sally, Tudi's girlfriend and the daughter of the local butcher, making her a member of one of the more well-to-do families in the neighborhood. Lucy is the "coolest chick in town," able to beat up on any fool who gets in her way, the smartest dresser, quick with a smart remark, and Blanca's best friend. Using the wedding as a focus, Ponce is able to create for the reader the preoccupations of each character: Cricket wants to be the meanest, toughest, coolest dressed *vato* [dude] in the barrio; Blanca wants the biggest wedding in the barrio; Lucy wants to be the coolest, best dressed chick in town; Tudi wants to survive, pay off his car, support his mom, and have a good time with Sally; Sally wants to be the nicest girl in town. Through the humorous adventures that include Blanca's job plucking turkeys, Cricket's constant fights, Tudi's fumbling, and Lucy and Blanca's search for the perfect wedding dress, Ponce also exposes the racism these teenagers face, the ignorance surrounding them, the poverty, the sexism, and above all the violence. Ponce has published another work, *Taking Control* (1987), a collection of stories about women. This is her first novel.

   The Last of the Menu Girls (1986) by Denise Chavéz is another story that also questions social values. The main character, Rocío Esquibel, links this loose collection of seven stories. In the first story we are introduced to Rocío by way of a document identifying her as a seventeen-year-old with little work experience; throughout the novel, Chavéz develops and fills in the "true" identity of Rocío. The first story describes Rocío, a "menu girl" (a person who hands out the meal checklist to patients in hospitals), and the patients she deals with. The second story, "Willow Games," recreates a child's world of play and the adventures the streets can provide an imaginative child like Rocío. In "Shooting Stars," Rocío speculates on what it means to pass from girlhood to womanhood. Here, as in Laura del Fuego's work, there is the ambiguity of "loving" women and celebrating women without the explicit claim of a lesbian identity. "Evening in Paris" treats the universal theme of a child's shattered illusions. Rocío has found the perfect Christmas gift for her mother, a small bottle of perfume, but her mother relegates it to the pile of other useless Christmas gifts she has received in the past. To Rocío this is a great personal tragedy. Chavéz depicts the anguish without patronizing the child, leaving Rocío her integrity. "The Closet" is a creative representation of a home and the individuals who inhabit it. Looking into the closets, Chavéz sinks into the heart of a female household: packed away in boxes and sitting on shelves are memories of the religious and sexual experiences of its members. "Space is a Solid" introduces other voices: Rocío's student, the student's mother, and Rocío's own confused and chaotic inner voice. The story involves the splintering of identity and Rocío attempting to keep sane by making tacos. It is a chaotic collage of voices, meant to be confusing. In the last story, "Compadre," the reader hears the voice of the handyman who is a *compadre* (the relationship of a child's parents to its godparents). This story explores the relationships between the family members: Rocío, her mother, her godfather, and her sisters. Rocío returns to her family, her neighborhood, and her home in order to write the story of her world.

Chavéz also explores the development of a writer; unlike del Fuego, who uses traditional chronology, or Corpi who begins with one story and flashes back to another story and then returns to her original story, Chavéz attempts a more fragmented history of the development of the author by using loosely connected short stories, a series of snapshots of the author's life. Chavéz freezes moments in

Rocío's life and describes them, usually through first person narration, though she does not always use Rocío as narrator. Like the other stories of developing writers, this one is also semi-autobiographical. Born in New Mexico, Chavez has written numerous plays and stories, including her latest novel, *Face of an Angel* (1994).

Across the Great River (1989), Irene Beltrán Hernández's first novel, is the story of a family illegally crossing the border into the United States. The main character, the ten-year-old Kata, gives a child's view of the events that have befallen her family: the illegal crossing, the disappearance of her father, the bullet that hits her mother, and the sanctuary found in Doña Anita's little ranch. This is also a story of a traditional healer, Doña Anita, who practices the old healing methods that have come from the indigenous populations of Mexico. Kata, her mother, and little brother move into town and are attacked by someone who thinks Kata's family has something valuable. (Kata holds in her possession a large heavy stone in a pouch hidden on her by her father.) Anita and Kata's mother are put in the hospital after the attack, and the children are taken to the Youth Center. The clash between Doña Anita, the traditional healer, and Doctor Mendez, a hospital physician, represents the cultural clash that Kata discovers in the U.S. Doña Anita and Kata's mother recover. Kata's mother wishes to return to Mexico. Anita takes the gold nugget Kata has been carrying and sells it for cash to return to Mexico and buy some land. Back in Mexico, Anita calls in some favors and gets Kata's father out of jail. He had gotten turned around when crossing the river and ended up swimming back into Mexico, where he was thrown in jail. At the end of the novel all is well, and everyone is returned to their traditional place in society.

The House on Mango Street (1984) by Sandra Cisneros is a collection of vignettes told through the eyes of Esperanza, a young child, as she writes in a journal. Based upon Esperanza's own experiences and thoughts as she is growing up on Mango Street, these vignettes of her family, neighborhood children, school adventures, and the every-day moments of an adolescent, represent childhood moments without adult introspection. For example, in one vignette, a neighbor's cousin comes driving up in a new Cadillac and offers everyone a ride. The police show up and everyone must get out of the car quickly. The car wrecks at the end of the street:

> The nose of that yellow Caddie was all pleated like an alligator's, and except for a bloody lip and a bruised forehead, Louise's cousin was okay. They put handcuffs on him and put him in the back seat of the cop car, and we all waved as they drove away. (25)

The naivete of the narrator allows the reader to supply her own political evaluation of the scene. Using a child's point-of-view, Cisneros uses the language of an adolescent to tell the stories, short, choppy sentences and limited vocabulary. Although the novel is written in a style appropriate for a young adult audience, the critique Cisneros provides of the violent world this child inhabits is clearly meant to educate more than just children. Children are beaten, cars are stolen, wives are abused, and the narrator is raped. While the narrator, Esperanza, is a naive innocent, she records more than she understands. The author, Cisneros, leaves the implications of this child's experiences up to the reader. Cisneros, also a poet, has a second collection of short stories, *Woman Hollering Creek* (1991).

The Mixquiahuala Letters (1986) by Ana Castillo is a collection of letters from one woman to another. Teresa writes to her friend, Alicia, whose responses we never see; Teresa sustains all the conversation between them. The two women meet in Mexico while enrolled in a summer cultural studies seminar. Teresa makes it very clear that she is of Mexican descent; however, we are never sure about Alicia. Teresa claims that Alicia is white—but only half white. The time sequence of the letters is also left ambiguous; the letters jump back and forth between their first trip to Mexico and their second trip. What is not ambiguous is the travel through Mexico and the men who entertain them. Their first trip through Mexico holds good memories; their second trip is emotionally and physically trying. During the second trip, Teresa falls in love with a wealthy entrepreneur who promises marriage. That promise is broken. Back in the U.S., Teresa and Alicia continue to struggle in relationships with men. When Alicia ends a relationship with her boyfriend, his response is to commit suicide. The theme of these letters is the relationships these women have with men and the relationship they have with each other. Castillo compares and contrasts the abusive treatment these women receive from white, Mexican, Chicano, and African-American men with the strong, supportive relationship the women have with each other.

Ana Castillo's collections of poetry include *Women Are Not Roses* (1984), *Otro canto* (1977), and *The Invitation* (1983). Her stories have appeared in numerous anthologies and journals. Her other novels include *Sapogonia* (1990) and *So Far From God* (1993).

Intaglio: A Novel in Six Stories (1990) by Roberta Fernández uses the narrator, Nenita, to hold the six stories together. Each story depicts one woman who represents culture and its diversity within a Mexican-American community set in a small Texas bordertown. Nenita tells the story of six women whose lives are the precursors to their daughters' and grand-daughters' Chicana feminism and how culture is reproduced. The work is an attempt to preserve the oral histories and stories of those women and to show their influence on the present generation of feminists.

Roberta Fernández calls herself a cultural worker who has prepared an anthology on Latina writers, *In Other Words* (1994).

The final work is more difficult. *Puppet* (1985) by Margarita Cota-Cárdenas is a self-proclaimed "Chicano" novel. Experimental, written mostly in non-standard Spanish with a few words and sentences in English, the novel tells the life and times of Puppet: a life of poverty, drugs, gangs, violence, and problems in school. A kid from the neighborhood who walks with a limp that goes unnoticed by most because he was so good looking, Puppet is killed by the police. The real story, however, belongs to those who are telling it; Puppet never speaks for himself. His friends, particularly one person, Pat Leyva, a writer, tell his story for him. She is from another part of town, of Mexican descent, speaks Spanish with an Anglo accent, and is a story teller. The search for Puppet's story becomes Pat's own story. The voices in this novel are pluralistic; each individual voice tells Puppet's story, each seeking the "real" Puppet. Cota-Cardenas is creating a world without a clear experience of what "actually" happened; the specific details are different for everyone. One of the fascinating elements of this novel is the language, the use of Spanish and English, the language of the streets Puppet came from.

Puppet is Margarita Cota-Cárdenas first novel, and she has in press two collections of poems, *Antimitos y contraleyendas* and *Marchitas de mayo: sones pa'al pueblo*.

Examples from these novels by Mexican-American women provide the material for my analysis of the forms, themes, and issues of this emergent canon. In "Toward a Mestiza Feminist Poetics," I describe and analyze a Chicana feminist poetics based on the work of Anglo feminist Elaine Showalter and poet-essayist Gloria Anzaldúa. Showalter's work provides (in modified form) a useful model for the development of a feminist literary tradition; Anzaldúa's *Borderlands/ La Frontera: The New Mestiza* (1987) provides the theoretical framework for some of the questions contemporary Chicana writers attempt to answer in their works. These include concepts of identity as represented in ethnic traditions, inscribed in language and informed by gender roles. Anzaldúa voices the contradictions in identity represented in Mexican-American culture. She evaluates traditional conceptions of female identity based upon a matrix of differences and contradictions.

"The Polictics of Culture" focuses on some of the emerging patterns in these novels: the assimilationist conception of ethnic and dominant culture; the accommodationist conception of the clash between the ethnic and the dominant culture; and the revisionist or revolutionary conception of a new culture characterized by the "borderland" identity.

In "The Politics of Language," I focus on language and formal innovation. The authors again fall into three categories: those who use traditional standard English, those who employ some bilingualism, and those who write in nonstandard forms of both English and Spanish. An author's relationship to standard English is a political one. Since English perhaps more clearly than anything else represents the dominant culture, the degree to which these authors find standard English adequate to articulate Mexican-American female identity and experience is a measure of their engagement with or opposition to cultural norms of the United States. Once again a pattern emerges wherein the assimilationist uses standard English, the accommodationist uses some bilingualism, and the revisionist disrupts and abandons standard forms.

"The Politics of Gender" is the study of representations of gender in Mexican-American culture. These representations are informed by the "feminine," the creation of a female identity grounded in traditional gender roles and characterized by a preoccupation with the needs of others, especially male members of the family. The "female" or critical exploration of traditional gender roles is represented by the conflicted character who recognizes the limitations of gender roles without offering an alternative. The projection of an alternative "feminist" position creates a new identity both informed by traditional gender roles and resistant to them.

Notes

1 Moraga uses the term "Chicana" to identify Mexican-American women. The terms used to identify Hispanics in the United States vary from region to region, culture to culture, and by political position. "Hispanic" is an umbrella term created by the U.S. Bureau of Census in order to identify individuals of the Spanish and Portuguese diaspora. "Latina" identifies women of Hispanic descent and also applies to individuals from Latin America. "Nuyorican" designates a Puerto Rican from New York. In *Breaking Boundaries: Latina Writings and Critical Readings* (1989), the editors, Asunción Horno-Delgado, Eliana Ortega, Nina M. Scott, and Nancy Saporta Sternback, in a footnote, discuss the diversity of terms and caution the reader:

> The term [Nuyorican] grew out of the fact that New York was the locus of the greatest number of Puerto Rican immigrants. Yet it should be pointed out that Puerto Ricans live all over the U.S. This is also a term with political implications of a separate identity from the U.S. and from the dominant culture of the Island. Not all Puerto Rican writers in the U.S. have adopted this term. Similarly, not all Mexican American writers will identify themselves as Chicanos, a term with political connotations stemming from the Chicano movement of the sixties. (xiii)

Chicana, as a term, now represents the obviously politicized Mexican American. Some individuals, however, do not recognize the term Chicano and hence use Mexican American.

2 Eliana Ortega and Nancy Saporta Sternbach acknowledge a similar "borrowing" in their essay, "At the Threshold of the Unnamed: Latina Literary Discourse in the Eighties" (1989):

> If it is possible to speak of a tradition in this current wave of Latino writing within the last twenty years, it is because of the existence of . . . . the discourse of U.S. women writers, most especially Black writers, which provide a female context. To this day Latina writers may express a debt to Black women writers. (18)

3 Moraga is discussing the following statement: we are ". . . committed to struggling against racial, sexual, heterosexual, and class oppression and see as our particular task, the development of integrated analysis and practice based upon the fact that the major systems of oppression are interlocking." The Combahee River Collective, "A Black Feminist Statement" (Hull, Scott, and Smith 1982), 13.

4   Adelaida R. Del Castillo in "Malintzin Tenépal: A Preliminary Look into a New
    Perspective" (1977) gives the history of La Malinche's name:
       It was the custom among the Mexicas (Aztecs) to give their children the
       name of the day on which they were born. Doña Marina was given the
       name "Malinalli" which corresponds to the 12th day of the Aztec month,
       possibly her birthday. [Gutierre] Tibón tells us that it then occured to
       Cortés that Malinalli's name was very similar to that of the Spanish virgin
       martyr, Santa Marina, and thus, had the priest christen her "Doña Marina."
       It is believed that the indios then distorted "Marina" to "Malina" for the
       simple reason that their language didn't possess the phoneme "r"
       (linguistically classified as a liquid) and replaced this sound with the
       phoneme "l" (also a liquid). The indios also added the suffix "tzin" to her
       name as an indication of their respect and affection for her. The Spaniards,
       in turn, changed "Malintzin" to "Malinche," interpreting the indigenous
       sound "tzin" for the Spanish "che." Doña Marina's family name was
       "Tenépal" and, to be sure, was well known in the province of Coatzacoalcos.
       (146)

5   Octavio Paz in *Labyrinth of Solitude: Life and Thought in Mexico* (1961) claims
    that Mexicans view La Malinche as the Mexican Eve and as the betrayer of her
    country.

6   Alarcón's essay in *This Bridge Called My Back* (1981), edited by Cherríe Moraga
    and Gloria Anzaldúa, provides an excellent discussion of contemporary poems
    about La Malinche.

7   Similar skepticism toward the women's movement can be found in the following:
    Sylvia Gonzales, "The White Feminist Movement: The Chicana Perspective"
    (1977); Theresa A. De Valdez, "Organizing as a Political Tool for the Chicana"
    (1980); Carmen D. Votaw, "Cultural Influences on Hispanic Feminism" (1981);
    Yvonne Yarbro-Bejarano, "Chicana Literature From a Chicana Perspective"
    (1988); and Irene Blea, *La Chicana and the Intersection of Race, Class, and
    Gender* (1992).

Chapter I

Toward a Mestiza Feminist Poetics

> Being bicultural is like living two lives, sometimes you're in one culture and
> sometimes you're in the other. When you're at home, all the beliefs and
> values you were raised with apply. When you go out to school or work, the
> other culture applies. I was getting an education to meet the demands of this
> [U.S. mainstream] society's culture. (Esperanza, "Siembra" 7)

These words appear in the first issue of the National Latina Health
Organization newsletter, signed "Esperanza" in the section entitled
"Siembra" [planting seeds]. This bilingual newsletter, written in
Spanish with an English translation of each article, is a new forum
and voice for a growing group of organized Latina women involved
with women's health issues. Esperanza echoes voices in the literary
works by Mexican-American women novelists. What these women
have in common is the experience of living in two cultures. There
are, however, inevitable tensions between the two worlds. The
border that separates them is not a clear line but a diffuse field of
tensions that divides one culture from the other. The ability to
inhabit and function in both is a major theme found among the works
of Mexican-American writers, and specific female experiences within
this bicultural existence are the concern of many Mexican-American
women writers.

One can understand and contextualize biculturalism in
literature in different ways. I choose to use American feminist theory
because an understanding of female identity as developed by Mexican-
American writers is the primary subject of my discussion. My
assumptions are based upon my personal experience as a member of
a Mexican-American community in the Southwest and an American-
educated feminist. Based upon those experiences and the lessons
that come from them, I have found Gloria Anzaldúa's work,
Borderlands/La Frontera: The New Mestiza—because it articulates

an indigenous feminism of the "borderland"—and Elaine Showalter's models of a "Feminist Poetics"—because her work represents a useful paradigm for the development of women's fiction—most helpful in my analysis of contemporary Mexican-American women's novels. These two authors together provide a language and framework from which these novels can be interpreted. Tey Diana Rebolledo in "The Politics of Poetics: Or, What Am I, A Critic, Doing in This Text Anyway?" calls for a theoretical framework that does not overwhelm and shadow the texts themselves.[1] I believe these theorists enrich but do not erase the literary texts.

I begin my discussion of the works of Mexican-American women novelists by arguing that some of these authors are moving toward a feminist Chicana understanding of women's experience. This "indigenous" feminism is best articulated by Gloria Anzaldúa and is characterized by a "borderland" identity.[2] The conflicts between the dominant and ethnic societies are often represented in these novels in three (sometimes overlapping) ways: an opposition to cultural norms (both the dominant and ethnic norms); an attempt at disruption or displacement of standard English; and a critique and revisualization of culturally assigned gender roles. These are the primary issues with which my analysis will be concerned.

How does a reader know that these novelists are moving toward an indigenous feminism? For this question, I find Elaine Showalter's concept of Anglo women's literary history very useful. Showalter first developed this model in *A Literature of Their Own: British Women Novelists from Brontë to Lessing* (1977), further defining it in "Toward a Feminist Poetics" (1979) and in her most influential essay, "Feminist Criticism in the Wilderness" (1981). Combining Showalter's framework with Gloria Anzaldúa's "borderland" identity, I describe and define an indigenous feminist critique of contemporary Mexican-American women novelists. I perceive these American authors, poets, and critics in dialogue with each other; bringing Anzaldúa, Showalter, and Mexican-American women novelists together further expands this feminist dialogue.

I. Understanding Showalter

Elaine Showalter's work continues to engage American feminist critical discourse in the development of what she calls a "gynocentric" theory of women's literature. In "Toward a Feminist Poetics," Showalter describes her sense of developmental stages in literature by women:

> When we go beyond Austen, the Brontës, and Eliot, say, to look at a hundred and fifty or more of their sister novelists, we can see patterns and phases in the evolution of a female tradition which correspond to the developmental phases of any subcultural art. (138)

Showalter's claim for developmental stages as a part of any literary subculture (comprised of non-canonical works, usually by women and minorities) is a very useful framework with which to understand literature created by Mexican-American women novelists. By first identifying and discussing Showalter's ideas and then modifying them in relation to the work by Gloria Anzaldúa in *Borderlands/La Frontera*, we can define an indigenous feminist theory that informs contemporary novels by Mexican-American women.

Showalter calls her three phases the "Feminine," "Feminist," and "Female" stages. Concerned with the need for equality and recognition by the mainstream literary culture, the first phase, the Feminine stage, is fairly predictable in terms of development for British women authors from 1840 to 1880: "women wrote in an effort to equal the intellectual achievements of the male culture, and internalized its assumptions about female nature" (138). A key idea is the claim that these authors, like the Brontës and Eliot, ". . . internalized [male culture's] assumptions about female nature." The internalization of society's assumptions and acceptance of those assumptions for oneself can also be called "assimilation." These authors were in fact attempting to assimilate into the prescribed male society in which their status as women was that of outsider. This attempt at assimilating into the literary male mainstream often required a change of name, e.g. George Eliot: "The distinguishing sign of this period is the male pseudonym, introduced in England in the 1840s, and a national characteristic of English women writers" (138).

This attempt at being just-like-one-of-the-boys also implies an acceptance of membership requirements. The desire for acceptance can take many forms. One can attempt to assimilate into clearly defined communities, informal groups, or any social unit that has distinct characteristics separating it from other groups. This desire for acceptance is ultimately a desire for power or self-actualization. By assimilating, one can gain power which appears to be concentrated in the dominant culture. But as we know, "assimilation" is never perfect, and even these early texts often subverted their own intentions—as we can read in Eliot's lament for Dorothea in the Epilogue of *Middlemarch*:

> Many who knew her, thought it a pity that so substantive and rare a creature should have been absorbed into the life of another, and be only known in a certain circle as a wife and mother. . . .
> But the effect of her being on those around her was incalculably diffusive: for the growing good of the world is partly dependent on unhistoric acts; and that things are not so ill with you and me as they might have been, is half owing to the number who live faithfully a hidden life, and rest in unvisited tombs. (611, 613)

The contradictions in that lament lead to the next phase.

Showalter's second stage, the Feminist phase, represents a critical stance toward male culture. Assimilation into the male literary club is no longer the primary goal of these authors--it is replaced by criticism of the male defined boundaries of literature: "In the Feminist phase, from about 1880 to 1920, or the winning of the vote, women are historically enabled to reject the accommodating postures of feminity and to use literature to dramatize the ordeals of wronged womanhood"(138). Showalter equates the beginnings of the feminist movement in this phase with the beginnings of a critique of patriarchy. No longer willing to accept society's assumptions without challenging them, women authors begin critiquing commonly held beliefs.

> The personal sense of injustice which feminine novelists such as Elisabeth Gaskell and Frances Trollope expressed in their novels of class struggle and factory life become increasingly and explicitly feminist in the 1880s, when a generation of New Women redefined the woman artist's role in terms of responsibility to suffering sisters. (138)

Challenging and critiquing long-held assumptions implies the system is incomplete because it fails to respond to the needs of much of the population. It is at this point that the criticism begins to sound like feminism. Half the population has either been ignored or woefully under-represented. The challenge is to change the system, not "join" it. Showalter claims that these authors, working within known systems in order to change them, are beginning to address the needs of women.

Important in distinguishing this stage is a willingness to work with the social and political institutions in order to correct their limitations. These authors assume that by rejecting parts of the dominant culture and bringing in new voices, change for the better can occur. In its resistance to the status quo, the second stage can be represented as the rebellious phase. It can also be understood as an accommodating phase, whereby the direct challenge to the system is actually muted because one is working within it and not outside it— resisting it still primarily on its own terms.

The third and final stage Showalter defines is the Female phase. This phase represents an attempt at defining a literary culture "outside" of patriarchy. It could also represent the revisionary stage of feminism. Women's culture is no longer defined merely in opposition to the patriarchal system but by female experience, "extending the feminist analysis of culture to the forms and techniques of literature"(139). In attempting to characterize and categorize British women's literary history, Showalter's final phase accounts for the radical writings by author's like Virginia Woolf and Dorothy Richardson. These authors "begin to think in terms of male and female sentences, and divide their work into 'masculine' journalism and 'feminine' fictions, redefining and sexualizing external and internal experience" (139). This new self-consciousness in women's literature includes the primacy of female experience in the literary imagination. It also ignores or dismisses male assumptions and tenets about literature and attempts to record a literature engendered by female experience.

Arguing that the authors she cites are attempting to write "outside" of patriarchy, Showalter claims that Woolf and Richardson were, in fact, precursors of the female phase. Criticized for a conception that authors can ever write outside of patriarchy, Showalter, in her later work, acknowledges that one cannot escape patriarchal language.[3] As the French feminists argue, language is "always/already" patriarchal, and the only place from which the Other can speak is the gaps and breaks in the Law of the Father.[4] In Showalter's discussion, woman's Otherness is represented by her disrupting patriarchal assumptions, not necessarily by creating a new language.

Gynocriticism, as Showalter calls her feminist theory, is acknowledged as one of the founding concepts of American feminist criticism. Jane Marcus in "Daughters of Anger/Material Girls: Con/Textualizing Feminist Criticism" (1988) provides an analysis of the tradition from which "American" feminists speak and its differences from "French" feminists. (Marcus uses quotation marks in labeling the two traditions in order to indicate the intellectual traditions from which the critics write, not their national status.) She carefully acknowledges the critical traditions that have contributed to the disparate sets of assumptions among American feminists and French feminists, as well as British feminists. Marcus then goes on to argue the following:

> This reaching out to the mass of readers, however much one may quibble over the choice of texts, is characteristic of the political nature of American feminism and its struggle to change institutions, unlike the French intellectual engagement with individual male thinkers, like Freud or Lacan. The writing of the American critic is aimed democratically at a very large audience of "common readers," not a small academic coterie, in a political gesture to change hearts and minds. (289)

After this high praise, however, Marcus does not ignore Showalter's limitations. *The New Feminist Criticism*'s "self-defined 'firstness'... is one of its dangers" (290):

> Aside from ignoring her contemporary predecessors, she ignores the past, and defines a mainstream feminism from personal practice, thereby relegating all "different" feminisms to the margins once again. . . . [This work is] a gesture backwards toward history rather than providing. . . current models . . . . (290)

For Marcus, the failure in Showalter's work is not in its overall theme but in its inattention to differences within feminism, its insufficient concern with issues of race, class, and sexual orientation.

Keeping Marcus' criticism in mind, I find Showalter's three-tier concept of the literary development of women writers useful beyond the discussion of British women writers. The three phases can be translated into three categories of contemporary Mexican-American women's literature. In order to do so, however, I must change a few of the assumptions upon which Showalter bases her work. The first assumption I would qualify is the concept of the phases as historical, developmental stages. In actuality, each phase is represented by contempory Mexican-American women authors; they exist and occur simultaneously, not merely as sequential phases. The authors I discuss are contemporaries of each other and hold views described in all three of Showalter's phases. The feminine phase, which describes an attempt at equality or assimilation, is an agenda still actively pursued by some of these authors. The second stage, the feminist phase, is defined by an author's critical stance towards assumptions society makes about appropriate femininity. Such a position involves especially a critique of femininity as defined by the patriarchy and, I argue, is a major theme among Chicana novelists.

The third and final stage, the female phase, represents an attempt to escape patriarchal assumptions about the feminine and to articulate experience from a female perspective. Showalter's language certainly assumes an ability to escape patriarchy and enter an autonomous physical state where a pure female perspective exists. I argue that this is in actuality a projected or "utopian" state of existence and not a part of actual experience. These stages are not necessarily progressive but dialectical, reflecting different aspects of all women's writing, whether contemporary or not.

Another aspect of Showalter's theory with which I disagree is her choice of labels for the second and third phases. I would argue that a more accurate description would call the second phase "female" and the third "feminist." Admittedly, the second phase is a critique of patriarchy, a critical stance taken by an author. But such a position represents only one part of the feminist agenda: not only does feminism critique patriarchy, but it also provides a framework for a *different* conception of existence. Thus, by labeling the second phase "feminist," Showalter has been rightly accused of narrowing and limiting feminism to the critique of patriarchy, concentrating on only half the agenda feminism traditionally has encompassed. If the final stage of development attempts to go beyond "imitation and protest," as Showalter states, and to open up the text, we enter into the political and philosophical realm. Consequently, the term "feminist," a broader political term, is more appropriate than the term "female," a biological term, for this final phase. Hence, in my descriptions of these three aspects of women's writings, I will use the categories feminine, female, and feminist.

II. American Feminism Expanded

Elaine Showalter's article, "Women's Time, Women's Space: Writing the History of Feminist Criticism" (1987), continues her discussion of gynocriticism. In that essay, Showalter does not abandon her previous conceptions about gynocriticism; rather, she situates it in response to the criticism from the Lacanian, Althusserian, and Derridean schools of feminist thought. Attempting to place her theoretical formulations of gynocriticism in a tradition "within women's time instead of as a subset of standard critical time," Showalter provides an alternative to the present mainstream critical discourses occurring in English departments throughout the United States. By removing American feminist criticism from traditional histories of mainstream criticism, Showalter gives a more accurate development of feminist criticism. The relegation of feminist criticism to the margins and footnotes of mainstream criticism devalues the contributions of feminism.

Refusing to continue the marginalization of feminism, Showalter defines and situates gynocriticism:

> Since 1975, feminist criticism has taken two theoretical directions, that of the Anglo-American focus on the specificity of women's writing I have called *gynocritics*, and that of the French exploration of the textual consequences and representations of sexual difference that Alice Jardine has named *gynesis*. . . . Gynocritics is, roughly speaking, historical in orientation; it looks at women's writing as it has actually occurred and tries to define its specific characteristics of language, genre, and literary influence, within a cultural network that includes variables of race, class, and nationality.
>
> Gynesis rejects, however, the temporal dimension of women's experience, . . . and seeks instead to understand the space granted to the feminine in the symbolic contract. . . . Another very striking aspect of gynesis is its dependence on male masters and male theoretical texts. (37)

Inclusion of the specific variables of "race, class, and nationality" and the focus on women's writing, identifies Showalter's continued allegiance to American feminist criticism as a pragmatic and concrete endeavor. Identifying the continental feminists with their tradition based upon the works of male theorists and male authors and rejection of "the temporal dimension of women's experience," Showalter succinctly differentiates the two schools of feminist thought.

Clear to a student of American feminist criticism and its traditions is the primacy of women's experience. This first assumption represents a difference between American feminists and the "continentals." The valorization of women's experience is also very much Gloria Anzaldúa's first assumption. As an American-trained feminist who has attempted in her work to push the boundaries of American feminism, Anzaldúa writes in Showalter's "women's time." Anzaldúa speaks from and for a woman's space drenched in the traditional discourse of American feminism *and* the variables of race, class, and nationality. In her book, *Borderlands/La Frontera*, Anzaldúa articulates a "new consciousness" represented by the Chicana. This work depends on a feminist conception of gendered identity within the matrix of culture, race, class, and sexual orientation. By grounding her feminism in the physical experience of Mexican-American women in the Southwest, Anzaldúa's discussion of an indigenous feminism is an example of Showalter's female phase, which I have renamed "feminist." Defining a new consciousness that inhabits the "borderland," Anzaldúa attempts to write—and to live—in what Showalter calls the "wild zone."

In "Feminist Criticism in the Wilderness," Showalter explores a historical discussion of the different literary traditions influencing feminism. Drawing on the work of anthropologist Clifford Geertz, Showalter identifies the space from which women's experience occurs separate from male experience as a wild zone, "the product or construction of cultural forces" (259). She draws a figure of two intersecting circles, each representing male and female experience respectively. The part of the female circle that does not intersect with the male circle is what Showalter identifies as the "wild zone":

> If we think of the wild zone metaphysically, or in terms of consciousness, it has no corresponding male space since all of male consciousness is within the circle of the dominant structure and thus accessible to or structured by language. In this sense, the "wild" is always imaginary; from the male point of view, it may simply be the projection of the unconscious. (262)

She offers a visual image of a space not occupied by patriarchy, foreshadowing the work of Gloria Anzaldúa and her conception of a "borderland."

III. Understanding Anzaldúa

In *Borderlands/La Frontera*, Anzaldúa claims that a new consciousness has emerged from the marginalized corners of a subculture in the United States. Like Showalter's wild zone, Anzaldúa's borderland is both a physical and metaphysical cultural construct. In this work, the borderland or *la frontera* becomes both the concrete, geographical space and the cultural symbolic space occupied by the new mestiza. Beginning with the history of Mexican culture, exploring the myths of the indigenous populations, moving in time between ancient history and yesterday, Anzaldúa attempts a large vision that encompasses a whole culture. She voices the marginalized history of this new mestiza in both prose and poetry, Spanish and English, factual and mythical documentation.

Concentrating first on the physical border that exists between the United States and Mexico, Anzaldúa describes its history, the signing of treaties, the battles waged, the people caught between two worlds—one, "first world" and the other, "third." She also introduces the concept of the "new mestiza." From a people of Indian and Spanish blood with the traditions of Mexico as part of their heritage, this new mestiza lives in the United States and occupies the borderland. Defined by the complicated relations between old traditions and modern technology, American individualism and Mexican conceptions of *familia*, a language of English, Spanish, and their idioms, "the convergence has created a shock culture, a border culture, a third country, a closed country" (11). The borderland becomes the symbol for this culture that is multicultural and yet a separate culture as well.[5]

Anzaldúa describes the necessity either to change the destructiveness of all societies or to be crushed by it. Introducing the "enemy" as patriarchy, homophobia, cultural tyranny, and oppressive organized religions, she details how this enemy hurts women, discriminates against homosexuals, commits cultural genocide, and silences individuals. Invoking Malintzin, the legendary mistress of Cortéz and first mother of an Indian and Spanish child, Anzaldúa uses this strong cultural symbol of a conquered society to represent silent and brutalized marginalized peoples. This powerful image is part of an invisible borderland culture that Anzaldúa attempts to make visible to the dominant society that marginalizes Anzaldúa's own identity. By invoking the image of Malintzin, Anzaldúa follows in the tradition of other Chicana poets who have re-imagined the image of La Malinche.

In the first part of her essay, Anzaldúa voices the limitations, brutalities, and injustices of life in the borderland. Seeking to understand and provide a change in this shock culture, Anzaldúa introduces what she sees as the major cause of destructive societies and describes the processes that need to occur in order to heal society. "Entering Into the Serpent" is the history of the split, the dualities in Western thought. Once again, invoking the mythologized past, Anzaldúa calls upon the ancient goddess of Mesoamerica, *Coatlalopeuh*, possessed of all qualities—good, bad, indifferent, strong, weak, wrathful, benevolent:

> The male-dominated Azteca-Mexica culture . . . divided her [*Coatlalopeuh*] who had been complete, who possessed both upper (light) and underworld (dark) aspects. . . .
> After the Conquest, the Spaniards and their Church continued the split *Tonantsi/Guadalupe*. They desexed *Guadalupe*, taking *Coatlalopeuh*, the serpent/sexuality, out of her. They completed the split begun by the Nahuas by making *la Virgen de Guadalupe/Virgen María* into chaste virgins and *Tlazolteotl/Coatlicue/la Chingada* into *putas*; into the Beauties and the Beasts. They went even further; they made all Indian deities and religious practices the work of the devil. (27-28)

For Anzaldúa, dual thinking has split the individual into an unhealthy creature. This dualism has continued to reproduce itself to become the dominant system of thought.

Echoing her friend and colleague Cherríe Moraga, "a woman with a foot in both worlds. . . . refus[ing] the split. . . . [and] feel[ing] the necessity for dialogue . . ." (*Loving in the War Years*, 58), Anzaldúa calls for a healing process to begin, the healing of the division in thoughts and spirit; she calls it the *Coatlicue* state—"the fusion of opposites" (47). The *Coatlicue* state is "duality in life, a synthesis of duality, and a third perspective—something more than mere duality or a synthesis of duality" (46). It is this third property that is difficult for Anzaldúa to define and explain since there is no clear language available. Language has been infected with the split. Anzaldúa uses English, Spanish, Nahuatl (an indigenous language spoken in Mexico), and the so called mixed language of the U.S. borderland to help her communicate the *Coatlicue* state. Marcela Lucero-Trujillo in "The Dilemma of the Modern Chicana Artist and Critic" prophetically understood what Anzaldúa is trying to do: "The modern Chicana, in her literature, tries to synthesize the material and spiritual conflict of her essence" (329). This synthesis of the split creates a new state that also has no easily accessible language.

Language, and not necessarily the standard forms, becomes one of the ways to heal the split, and storytelling is central to the process. Translated into a written form, the oral tradition is another attempt to erase the destructive split that marginalizes the border culture. By healing the split, a borderland inhabitant that constantly must adjust to the conflicts of dualities may become whole.

After the process of healing is completed a new consciousness is formed, which Anzaldúa describes as "*La conciencia de la mestiza.*" In this conception, we find Anzaldúa's comprehension of an indigenous feminism. Based upon the experience of living in the borderland, informed by the cultural past, and conscious of feminist values, Anzaldúa claims a new subjectivity: "From this racial, ideological, cultural and biological cross-pollinization, an 'alien' consciousness is presently in the making—a new *mestiza* consciousness, *una conciencia de mujer* [a woman's conscience]. It is a consciousness of the Borderlands" (77).Because of the constant interaction between the dominant culture and the subculture, ethnic or gendered, the new mestiza must deal with "a cultural collision." The traditional responses to divisions are not healing:

> But it is not enough to stand on the opposite river bank shouting questions, challenging patriarchal, white conventions. A counterstance locks one into a duel of oppressor and oppressed; . . . both are reduced to a common denominator of violence. The counterstance refutes the dominant culture's view and beliefs. . . . Because the counterstance stems from a position of authority—outer as well as inner—it's a step towards liberation from cultural domination. But it is not a way of life. (78)

Anzaldúa argues that traditional responses to problems challenge patriarchy in a way reminiscent of Showalter's second stage of rebellion without revision. In that stage, patriarchy is the enemy but the response is still dependant upon the opposition. Nothing new is created. It is still only a rebel's cause.

Refusing to accept a modified status quo and challenging cultural assumptions are not enough for Anzaldúa. She wants an active alternative that escapes and transcends traditional thought patterns. She assigns this role to the new mestiza:

> The work of *mestiza* consciousness is to break down the subject-object duality that keeps her a prisoner and to show in the flesh and through the images in her work how duality is transcended. . . . A massive uprooting of dualistic thinking in the individual and collective consciousness is the beginning of a long struggle, but one that could, in our best hopes, bring us to the end of rape, of violence, of war. (80)

Like Showalter, Anzaldúa believes social and cultural change can occur only when "imitation and protest" are transcended. This next stage or state is not just a rebel's attack but a revolutionary position. Unlike Showalter, who envisions the answer within the separate world of female experience, Anzaldúa does not see separation between female and male culture as an answer. Anzaldúa's new mestiza is a symbol of questioning relationships to power as well as trying to transcend the dichotomy of powerful/powerless. "The possibilites are numerous once we decide to act and not react" (Anzaldúa 79).

The merging of Anzaldúa's new mestiza with Showalter's three phases provide a framework from which Mexican-American women novelists can be studied. This framework informs my discussions of issues of culture, language, and gender in the following chapters.

Notes

1 Tey Diane Rebolledo in "The Politics of Poetics" gives a humourous account of how texts can be overwhelmed by theory:

> I would say a typical talk could be summarized in the following way: the speaker begins, "The paper will focus on the ideology of cultural practice and its modes of signifying." S/he then spends the twenty minutes discussing how the works of whatever theoretical greats s/he selects will define, inform and privilege the work s/he is doing. Such names as Jameson, Said, Williams, Hall, Burke and other contemporary *meros*, *meros* (mostly male) will be invoked over and over. The speaker is then sent a note by the chair of the panel that there is not time left. And whatever the Chicano/a writing or phenomena that was to be discussed is quickly summarized in two minutes. The talk is over. We have talked so much about theory we never get to our conclusion nor focus on the texts. By appropriating mainstream theoreticians and critics we have become so involved in intellectualizing that we lose our sense of our literature and therefore our vitality. This priority of placing our literature in a theoretical framework to "legitimize" it, if the theory overshadows it, in effect undermines our literature or even places it, once again, in a state of oblivion. Privileging the theoretical discourse de-privileges ourselves. (131)

2 I use the term "indigenous feminism" because I need a concept that acknowledges a feminism informed by an individual's specific circumstances. Cherríe Moraga in *This Bridge Called My Back* identifies indigenous feminism this way: "Each [contributor to the book] identifies herself as a feminist, but draws her feminism from the culture in which she grew" (xxiv). Rebolledo has a similar concept that I would identify as indigenous feminism:

> I believe that our critical discourse should come from within, within our cultural and historical perspective. This is not to say that I am advocating limited, regional, small-minded descriptive literary analysis. But I think we should internalize and revolutionize theoretical discourse that comes from outside ourselves, accepting that which is useful and discarding that which is merely meant to impress. ("The Politics of Poetics" 137)

3 Several feminist theorists have addressed this problem from a number of perspectives. The most useful include: Nelly Furman, "The Politics of Language: Beyond the Gender Principle?" (1985), 64; Gayle Greene and Coppelia Kahn, "Feminist Scholarship and the Social Construction of Woman," (1985), 25; Adrienne Munich, "Notorious Signs, Feminist Criticism and Literary Tradition,"

(1985), 244; Toril Moi, *Sexual/Textual Politics: Feminist Literary Criticism* (1985) 75-80; Luce Irigaray, *Speculum of the Other Woman* (1985) and *This Sex Which is Not One* (1985); and Hélène Cixous, "The Laugh of the Medusa," (1980).

4 Irigaray, *Speculum of the Other Woman*, 32-34 and Cixous, "The Laugh of the Medusa," 257.

5 Anzaldúa's descriptions have consistently been identified as examples of the postmodern moment. That construction is accurate; however, I prefer the language of Anzaldúa to language of postmodern theory to describe that specific space.

Chapter II

The Politics of Culture

Among the common themes in the work of Mexican-American women novelists, one of the most central is a need to describe the cultures from which they emerge and to locate their characters in relation to those cultures. All of the authors in this study create characters grounded in specific traditions and beliefs associated with Mexican-American communities. In the discussion of relationships between individual characters and culture, we can describe three major categories roughly parallel to the developmental phases in Showalter's paradigm: an *assimilationist* conception of the relations between ethnic and dominant cultures; an *accommodationist* conception of that relationship; and a *revisionist* conception of a new culture characterized by a "borderland" identity.

The assumptions that identify an assimilationist view of culture include an essentialist belief that cultures are fundamentally different, and those differences are identifiable; that a culture can be defined and its characteristics categorized; that choices can be made as to what characteristics of a culture an individual will accept or discard; and that cultural norms are rarely problematic (norms exist and are either accepted or rejected). These assumptions make it possible for clear distinctions (or at least the illusion of clear distinctions) between two apparently distinct cultures, one "Mexican" and one "American." Internalizing the values of one culture in opposition to the other, characters manifest an awareness of both and represent choices between them. For assimilationist characters, one culture becomes the acceptable norm, the other inferior or

FC

devalued. They privilege American mainstream culture over Mexican by everything from mundane food choices (hot dogs instead of tamales) to the desire for an education in an American university. American culture becomes appropriate, and Mexican culture is transformed into the "other": choosing to watch a football game over a soccer game; listening to American rock music instead of Mexican music; demanding English be spoken at home and not Spanish represent some of the ways a literary character becomes assimilated. To assimilate is to take on cultural characteristics that were not originally a part of one's culture of origin and to repress or deny aspects of one's ethnic identity which are marked as deviant by the dominant culture.[1]

The accommodationist concept of culture begins with some of the same assumptions about culture as the assimilationist: distinct cultural differences can be categorized and defined, and cultural norms are relatively clear. The accommodationist, however, does not privilege one culture over another. Attempting to resolve clashes, to find complementary values, and to take from both cultures, the accommodationist constantly negotiates the tensions between them. When two mutually exclusive cultural conceptions clash—for example, individualism versus *familia*—the accommodationist attempts to combine the two values and not reject one for the other. An accommodationist may, for example, acknowledge individualism as a value in the public sphere (work and school) and *familia* in the private sphere (marriage and intimate relationships), leading a difficult double cultural existence. A character like Delia in Corpi's *Delia's Song* can have both worlds: the family in the barrio and the community at Berkeley. She can straddle two very different worlds and expect to function in both. Home is tranquil and traditional:

> In Monterey, Delia spent most of her time reading, taking long walks, helping her aunt and mother make skirts and blouses for her to take to Berkeley, while listening to her aunt's lively stories about their family in Mexico. (57)

The campus, on the other hand, is a hodge-podge of cultures competing for attention:

> As always, Hubert The Preacher and a black man were arguing about sin
> and hell, surrounded by a hollering crowd under the steady autumn rain;
> Hare Krishna followers chanted, oblivious to the howling of dozens of dogs
> loose on the campus; an emaciated man played his violin for nickels; students
> played chess under the protection of their umbrellas at Ludwig's Fountain;
> dazed-eyed hippies sprawled on the Student Union steps next to their
> knapsacks. (27)

Similarly, in del Fuego's *Maraville*, Las Belltones, Cece's gang,
represents a surface combination of American and Mexican teen
popular culture.

> The initiation rites: no make-up for a month; no talking to guys for a
> week; wearing blouses and sweaters backwards for one week; doing chores
> and running errands at the club meetings and social events until someone
> new had been initiated. (11)

An accommodationist conception does not try to resolve the split
caused by dualities—that split is accepted. There is no fundamental
challenge to binary opposites, just an adjustment to accommodate
the two halves.

A revisionist conception of culture works from different
assumptions about culture than those of the assimilationist and
accommodationist. For the revisionist, cultures cannot be distinctly
categorized as one kind or another; cultural norms are not stable and
essential, but unstable and problematic; and a "third space" emerges
that represents not merely the sum of two cultures, but a more
dialectical one, transcending rigid dualities. It is this third space,
where at least two traditional cultures can exist and still be one, that
is represented by Anzaldúa's "borderland"—a place where nothing
is marginalized and all experience included, a new "species" which
has its own sets of norms and characteristics. The assimilationist's
and accommodationist's vision of culture is transcended in this third
space, a projected or utopian world. Denise Chávez in *The Last of the
Menu Girls* finds this third world in her neighborhood where English
and Spanish are spoken side-by-side, where *Gone With the Wind* is
discussed while offering tamales to a compadre, where the tensions
of two worlds are blurred to become one.

"I tell her, Roque, just write one *Gone With the Wind*. That's all. Just one. You don't have to go anywhere. Not down the street. Not even out of this house. There's stories, plenty of them all around. What do you say, Rocio?" "Mas tamales, anybody?" I said." Compadre?" (190)

Contemporary Mexican-American women novelists portray culture in all three forms: the assimilationist wants to integrate into the dominant culture; the accommodationist attempts to negotiate the two cultures and bring them together; the revisionist sees a third one formed by the two cultures, larger than the sum of its parts. These novels sometimes characterize an assimilationist concept in order better to define an accommodationist position, and no work is purely accommodationist or assimilationist. I want to argue additionally that a *feminist* Chicana conception of culture is best represented by Gloria Anzaldúa's borderland "mestiza" culture.

My discussion of assimilation focuses on two examples: the choices characters make between folk medicine and mainstream medicine; and institutionalized education as a tool for assimilation. Accommodationist views of culture are best exemplified in issues connected with religion. Examples of revisionist ideologies are represented as "moments" in the novels, moments that are glimpsed but not sustained.

I. Assimilationism

The most representative example of an assimilationist conception of culture among contemporary Mexican-American women's novels is Irene Beltrán Hernández' work, *Across the Great River*. Within this narrative, characters, even those of Mexican descent, follow either Mexican customs or American ones; no real mix takes place. A Mexican who lives in the United States may still hold Mexican values unless she/he choose to assimilate into the American mainstream, but characters who assimilate into the dominant culture leave behind their culture of origin. This novel asks the reader to compare the mainstreamed doctor, Dr. Mendez, and the indigenous healer, Anita, as manifestations of two separate cultural values between which Kata and her family are caught.

The story focuses on Kata and her family crossing the border illegally. Separated from her father and with her mother wounded, Kata must take responsibility for herself and her baby brother as they are housed by Doña Anita, the community healer. Anita represents the old indigenous customs rooted in Mexican folk values and medicine.

Kata, the narrator, begins her portrayal of Doña Anita with an image of fear. She and her family have just been dragged over to Anita's home, and Kata's first view of her occurs late at night.

> A bulky woman, carrying a small lantern, steps out onto the porch. Her massive body is covered by a long white gown. She quickly raises the lantern and peers out. I can see one big eye that opens and shuts like that of an owl, and I grab Mama tightly. (16)

Anita's initial appearance is of a spirit or monster-like creature that frightens Kata into calling her a "horrid woman" with "fowl breath" (16-17). But Kata, worried about her mother, must admire this woman's skills:

> I stand watching the old one work. Her hands move rapidly from one jar to another and never seem to stop. I marvel at her speed for such a fat woman. Occasionally, she closes both eyes and bends down to listen to Mama's chest, then she grunts as if she were about to throw up. Never once does she look up from her work, I watch very closely as her healing hands tend to Mama's wound. She truly has a gift from God, I decide. (17-18)

Doña Anita embodies traditional Mexican values, which are a combination of indigenous and Catholic religious beliefs. Anita is a *curandera*, though the term is never directly applied to her perhaps because of its association with evil as well as good, a level of cultural ambivalence this novel does not endorse: "'No, I am not a witch. I am a healer, and a seer. I work for God, not for the devil. Remember, there is a difference'" (26). The combination of "healer" and "seer" partially defines a *curandera*, which traditionally is associated with both the light and dark forces of indigenous spirituality.

The Spanish term, however, has many other implications that the narrative strips from it by specifically defining Anita as a healer and seer who "works for God," avoiding the more slippery implications of the *curandera*.[2] Gloria T. Hull describes the power "of the healer/root woman/curandera/medicine woman. Though she was/is generally kept from sacred objects and patriarchal ruling places, she is a powerful figure who appears in countless tales, reminiscences, stories, and poems" (*Reading Literature* 22). By simplifying and distinguishing easily between good and bad ("God" and "devil"), the narrative can to a certain extent control the implications of Doña Anita as simple folk healer and not as a powerful, mystical *curandera*, maintaining the stable dualisms necessary to a cultural assimilationist. Introducing Anita as someone on the side of good, whose spiritual skills as seer and healer are not inspired by evil, Beltrán Hernández offers a nonthreatening folk healer; Anita's other skills as interpreter of dreams and forecaster of the future appear innocuous, unlike the more dynamic and uncomfortable cultural image of a *curandera*. The reader can accept Anita's mystical skills because they are presented benignly:

> "Why do you know so much about dreams?" I ask, not making much sense out of her rattling on in such a way.
> She rises, goes over to the closet and she pulls out a small book. "This is a dream book and it tells all about dreams and their outcome. I have studied it faithfully because I feel it is part of every person alive." (31)

The initial awe and mystery surrounding Anita in Kata's eyes and usually associated with the *curandera* figure are gradually demystified as Doña Anita's prophetic and healing powers are transformed into her role as everybody's grandmother, a large, down-to-earth woman who takes care of people. The potential contradictions in her character are evaded.

The social skepticism of most Anglo communities for nonphysical experience is represented by another minor character, Doctor Mendez. Initial fear of Doña Anita's skills by Kata parallels Mendez' initial distrust of Anita. Attempting to introduce Mexican culture to an audience unfamiliar with that culture, Beltrán Hernández emphasizes its separateness from American mainstream culture. Characters tend to be either Mexican or assimilated American, as is Mendez. Anita does explain that Mexicans born in the United States still keep their Mexican heritage, but she focuses more on difference than on continuity:

> "Sometimes I [Kata] forget that I'm no longer in Mexico."
> Anita chuckles, "That's very easy to do in this little town with its plaza and market which are so much like the ones in Mexico. You see, the people here are mostly Mexicans, but they are born on this side of the river and that

> makes them Mexican-Americans. You were born on the other side of the river
> and that makes you a native Mexican."
>   "But Anita," I argue, "everyone speaks Spanish."
>   "Language has nothing to do with it. There is a government that runs
> Mexico and there is a different government that runs the United States." (58)

The difference between Mexicans in Mexico and those in the United States can be represented by their governments; cultural identity is minimized. As with the easy difference between good and evil, this difference between Mexicans and Americans oversimplifies some very complicated relationships. Reductionism is the price one pays when demanding the clear and simple lines between two cultures. Ambiguities and shades do not survive in a so-called black and white world, which is the world of the assimilationist. In order to privilege one culture, the other must be muted and, hence, colonialism can best exist in a simplistic, dualistic world. The title of the novel reinforces this clear division between cultures. To cross the Rio Grande is to cross into another world. For as much as Kata admits her confusion about no longer being in Mexico and the implied blurring of cultural distinctions, Anita brushes those ideas aside in the interest of difference. Mexico and the United States are both reduced to lines on maps, and one can cross to the other; even though they may feel the same—they are different. It is the simplistic assertion of difference that allows for assimilationist consciousness.

Those Mexicans who have assimilated, like Doctor Mendez, hold "American" values. Mendez maintains his skepticism about Anita's skills throughout the novel.

> "I would have recovered sooner had I had some of my own medicine."
>   The doctor stiffens and says, "We study two distinct arts that accomplish
> the same healing goal, Doña Anita."
>   . . . "If she had my herbal tea she would already be walking around!"
>   The doctor bites his lips and says, "Please, Doña Anita. May I remind
> you that this is my consultation with Kata." (83-84)

Mendez consistently responds to Doña Anita with a patronizing attitude. In order to cure Kata, who has had the evil-eye cast upon her, Mendez and Anita must work together, and only after that incident does Mendez learn to appreciate Anita without necessarily understanding her.

"You see, the doctor and I [Mendez' housekeeper] had late coffee together and he explained everything after she [Anita] left. It seems he thinks a lot of her in a mysterious sort of way."

"Mysterious? What is that?" [Kata asks]

"It means that he likes her and respects her, but can't really figure her out. You know, like you really can't figure out all the facts about God." (115)

This discussion typifies the relationship between Mexican culture and American culture in this novel. A character or audience can "like" another culture without having to understand it. The interaction between cultures takes the same form as the interaction between Doña Anita and Doctor Mendez. Beltrán Hernández appears to assume that an assimilated reader may not be willing to give up her skepticism but must at least acknowledge a grudging respect for another person's beliefs. As long as there is a recognizable division between the two of them, Anita and Mendez can coexist in the same community without having to accept the other one's beliefs. Anita will always remain the "other" for Doctor Mendez, even after they share a moment when they actually work together. In this scene, "assimilationist" ideologies slide into accommodationist ones; distinctions are maintained but difference is tolerated. This is not a new partnership and the moment is not sustained. What makes this work an assimilationist narrative is the fact that the accommodationist moment is undercut immediately. After working together to heal Kata, Mendez and Anita fail to realize that their combined energy is powerful. Neither character is willing to relinquish his or her separate positions in the community. For Mendez to seek Anita's medical assistance would be to question the privileged status of mainstream medicine and to create something potentially revisionist.

For Doctor Mendez, the whole experience with Kata evolves into a learning process. He has tried to live in both worlds, Mexican and American, by marrying a Mexican woman he did not love because it was what was expected by their families. The narrative implies that it was inappropriate of Mendez to try to live in both worlds after he has assimilated into the American value system. The marriage represents the combining of the two separate cultures—in this novel, dooming it to failure. All Mendez really wants is his American girlfriend he had to break up with when he had succumbed to his family's wishes. And Kata realizes Doctor Mendez' attempt to live in two worlds is impossible.

At the end of the novel the balance has been restored: Anita continues to live according to her traditions, Kata returns to Mexico, Mendez is dating his American girlfriend again, and his wife, who was also unhappy with the marriage, has returned to Mexico. Mendez is back in his appropriate space outside Mexican traditions. Anita chooses not to assimilate but to continue her role as *curandera*. There are no reprisals, only rewards, for choosing appropriately, as long as a character does not try to mix the two cultures, does not attempt a hybrid existence.

The clear lines and boundaries between cultures, symbolized by Beltrán Hernández in the "Great River," appear as natural and distinct in other works as well. In *Last of the Menu Girls* by Denise Chávez, the main character, Rocío, begins by attempting to assimilate into the dominant American culture in New Mexico. Rocío finds herself at the hospital doing a summer work-study job, preparing to enter college and leaving her community behind. Education is often seen as the most direct form of assimilation into the dominant community. The stories in *Menu Girls* weave backwards in time to the main character's childhood in a Mexican-American community. When the narrative turns to Rocío's graduate program, the reader realizes the degree to which the main character has assimilated into the dominant culture. At this point in the narrative, Rocío's emotional balance has been completely upset.

There is a significant time lapse between the stories of Rocío's adolescence and teen years and her life in graduate school. In "Space is a Solid," the many narrative voices are identified by their names as section dividers. When Rocío begins hers, we get the first hint of trouble. "It was at this time that my hands started turning blue" (103). Struggling with her M.F.A. program, teaching, and surviving as a poor student, Rocío is emotionally exhausted:

> "My hands are blue. My hands are blue. Loudon, my hands are blue."
> "Your hands are blue?" he says
> "God, my hands are blue! Loudon, I have to get out of this elevator."
> "Two floors to go!" Padded hysteria with two floors to go. (105)

Surrounded by the pressures of graduate school, student poverty, work in the costume department, and absorbed in a world of Anglos, Rocío finds herself with an "illness that crept up my arm, immobilizing

goodness and filling me with dread, inquietude and paranoia . . ."
(106), an illness clearly symbolic of her cutural displacement.

Nita Wembley, Rocío's landlord, represents for Rocío much
of the "madness" of the Anglo world. In search of an apartment,
Rocío meets Mrs. Wembley who is as unkempt as Rocío feels:

> "Now, you forget the curlers and the clothes and look at me. Look at
> me. Real close. See anything wrong?"
> "No, I . . . no . . ."
> "Miss Esquinel, I don't have no breasts."
> "You . . ."
> "I am without the breasts the good Lord gave me. First Kari Lee and
> then, well, can you see, Miss Esquinel, after a life of working hard, God should
> send me this tribulation from the land of Cain."
> "I'm . . ."
> "Oh no, no, no, no . . . don't you be sorry. Sorry ain't enough. After all
> these years, sorry ain't enough. Now, to look at me, anyone would see a
> normal woman. Do you know what it's like to have your female flesh cut away
> from you? Now I worked hard, I moved us from nowhere to the Oak Hill
> Estates. We got a nice fancy house full of pretty things and Cloyd handles all
> the skyscraper's accounts and we give to the Drama Factory. We are patrons.
> We belong to the 100 Club. Miss Esquinel, I believe in dreaming yourself
> something that you ain't." (115)

The disfiguring mastectomy is linked to Mrs. Wembley's pathetic
dreaming beyond her social class and reminds Rocío of what she is
doing in the drama program. In many ways Mrs. Wembley represents
the community into which Rocío is attempting to assimilate. The
scarred emotional life of a Mrs. Wembley represents Rocío's own
dreaming: to live in a nice neighborhood, to have nice things, to be
patrons of the arts—these embody many of the goals of assimilation.

Miserable and unable to function in either world, Rocío
returns to her old neighborhood to find a way to bring the two
worlds she inhabits together. The individualism demanded in the
dominant Anglo community is juxtaposed to the responsibilities of
family in the Mexican-American community. Trying to balance both
worlds, Rocío is pushed to her emotional limits. One world is
completely alienating, making Rocío feel totally vulnerable; the other
is so suffocating in its nurturing insistence that Rocío is overwhelmed,
in an emotional tailspin, and paralyzed by the divisions. In the midst
of dealing with the pressures, Rocío finds strength in a "borderland"
moment:

> "Maybe you should lie down," I [Loudon] said, and she was still crying.
> "No, no, no, if I lie down I'll die. I don't want to die. I have to make tacos." (133)

Making tacos keeps Rocío together. "'If it weren't for the tacos, Loudon, I don't know *how* I could have made it'" (134). This novel unlike *Across the Great River*, suggests that cultural identity, represented here by "making tacos," can be a source of strength, and that the process of assimilation is conflicted and never complete.[3]

    The Last of the Menu Girls represents assimilationist conceptions of culture: the idea of stable cultural difference with identifiable characteristics for two cultures; the impossibility of being a member of both worlds; and the assumption that it is better to choose one than to try and be in both. *Trini* by Estela Portillo Trambley begins similarly in an assimilationist ideology but moves more successfully into accommodating the contradictions involved in two cultures.

II. Accommodationism

    As accommodation supersedes assimilation as a goal or necessity, stable cultural boundaries are blurred and combined and the tensions between values in conflict can be at least partially resolved. The end product of the accommodationist model is cultural pluralism. Original cultural norms once compromised are not necessarily negated but subordinated in the service of a larger value. For example, individualism can be subordinated to the cultural value of *familia*, without erasing entirely the needs of the individual subject; the two are held in tension. Accommodationist narratives make it easy to slip in and out of the pluralist and assimilationist conceptions of culture because these narratives have similar initial assumptions about culture.

    This is best represented in *Trini* by Portillo Trambley's depiction of Catholicism as an example of how culture manifests itself in community traditions. One of the strongest characteristics of the Mexican community is its ritual understanding of Catholicism. The Catholicism practiced by most Mexicans has been heavily influenced by the indigenous practices of Central America. The tensions that divided indigenous spiritual beliefs from Catholicism were blurred as Catholicism came to dominate in the New World.

Trini's life story includes a historical analysis of the general development of Catholicism's acceptance in the hearts of the indigenous populations. The novel explores the importance of the fact that Catholicism was the original religion of the conqueror not the conquered, that the spread of Catholicism and the church's overwhelming success in bringing it to Central and Latin America are unique in the history of Catholic missionary work. Portillo Trambley traces the mythic story of religion forced upon the native peoples.

Trini's aunt, Tía Pancha, demands that the three children in the family become Catholics. She enters Trini's central Mexico valley as an angel of God, bringing salvation and cleanliness to what she envisions as young pagans. Tía Pancha represents a new life for her family. She brings order to disorder, cleanliness to filth, and bread to those who had never tasted it.

> Tía Pancha had stormed into their lives ten months before, well supplied with her plaster saints, religious calendars, crucifixes, scapularies, missals, clothespines, a scrub board, and a huge tina. Never had they seen such a tub. (36)

To Trini all these things are good, and they make the house a little more pleasant. Trini, however, has a few doubts. She likes the order and cleanliness, the white bread is a new meal to her, but Trini does not feel fully comfortable with this new God.

> I wish I understood the God Tía Pancha brought with her from San Mateo, thought Trini. She had never seen such passion for a God before. . . .
>   Trini remembered Tía Pancha's other passion, cleanliness. Right next to Godliness! Demanding the same frenzy. Aside from all this Tía Pancha was a loving, kind woman who showed it in many ways. (35-36)

The combination of devout Catholicism and nurturance provides the vehicle for acceptance by the children of this new religion. Overwhelmed, the children quickly and devoutly follow the commands of their aunt. They learn to prepare themselves for their first communion, bake bread, clean themselves every day, attend mass every Sunday, and forget the gods of the valley. Trini acknowledges that her way of life is disappearing from their valley: "It seemed as if many things that mattered were being erased from her life, forbidden by her aunt's beliefs"(38). She gradually realizes that she cannot give up the special relationship she has to the valley in exchange for Catholic prayers. "I am the valley, Trini decided, more than a Christian"(38). So while she learns the prayers and commits to the appearance of Catholic piety, Trini never loses her initial belief of the amorphous gods of her valley.

Finally finding the right combination of Catholic and indigenous rituals that allows for both of her worlds to be worshipped is not easy for Trini. Eventually, however, she accommodates the two traditions, allowing her to acknowledge and accept a dual religious heritage. When her family comes across a small town where the spring blessings are being performed Trini recognizes the kind of religion that does not alienate her.

> She walked up to an altar and watched girls strew corn leaves before it. On the altar was a statue of the Virgin Mary and a brown clay figure of the goddess Tonantzín. Trini felt Tía Pancha's grip on her arm, a questioning frown on her face. Trini knew she did not approve of a pagan goddess being placed next to the Virgin Mary. The four-breasted goddess of fertility looked like a lump of earth compared to the pretty painted little Virgin. Something pulsed in Trini, a secret preference for the brown goddess that seemed to gather strength in the sun and open air. Tonantzín was like the old ahau of Bucoyu, a spirit sprung from the earth. (73)

Realizing that she has come across a ritual that matches her beliefs, Trini also feels the disapproval radiating from her Catholic aunt. Asked to choose between this ceremony and the Catholicism of Tía Pancha, Trini is forced into making a choice:

> Trini stood, unsure. She wanted to be part of the chanting, the music, the benediction. She looked toward Tía Pancha, who stood waiting for her, Buti and Lupita by her side, then turned and looked toward the altar. Tonantzín was smiling at her! She sat down again and joined in the chant without looking back at Tía Pancha. (74)

Trini feels she has finally found the answer to a question she did not even know she had been asking. Trying to assimilate into traditional Catholicism, Trini finds she would be denying a part of herself. The ritual allows Trini to recognize herself in Tonantzín, the earth goddess. Like Tonantzín, Trini is in search of a valley where the family can plant seeds and grow life. Tonantzín represents the goodness that comes from the earth and fills one of Trini's needs.

The ability to enter a ritual that acknowledges and does not denigrate the indigenous experience and still includes the Catholic beliefs represents a moment of resolution for Trini which symbolizes a greater cultural merging.

Similarly, in *Maravilla*, Laura del Fuego creates a character who has visions of Saint Teresa. Cece, in her visions, accommodates her modern world within a Catholic tradition. St. Teresa appears as any other Mexican woman:

> "Who are you?" I asked, even though I knew.
> "Do you es-speak es-Spanish?" She sounded just like great-aunt
> Rebecca.
> "A little," I said. "I mean, *un poquito*."
> "*Soy Teresa de Avila*."
> "That's what I thought," I mumbled.
> "*Que año es*? she asked.
> "What?"
> "Time, what time eet ess?" (5-6)

Cece dusts off the old picture of St. Teresa and puts it in her room in order to continue talking to her. Her bridging mystical Catholicism and modern consciousness is similar to Trini's amalgam of indigenous and Catholic rituals; a pluralism of experience flourishes and cultural differences merge.

One of the assumptions about culture made by both accommodationist and assimilationist ideologies acknowledges religious beliefs as fundamental to Mexican and Mexican-American culture. Catholicism becomes inseparable from Mexican traditions, and any celebration of cultural heritage includes a veneration of Catholicism. The American ideal of separation of church and state is genuinely "foreign" to Mexican consciousness. While the Mexican government officially acknowledges itself as an atheistic state, in actuality, the Catholic church is one of the most dominant powers affecting Mexican societal values. Religion cannot be separated from culture in Mexican society. In fact Mexican-American authors depend upon clearly identifiable Catholic characteristics to distinguish Mexican culture from American culture. Many of the narratives assume that a large portion of the audience will be Protestant-influenced readers, to which Catholicism must be "justified."

One of the clearer examples of Mexican-influenced traditions involves the idea of lavish celebration. Mary Helen Ponce in *The Wedding* fully realizes how foreign her elaborate wedding appears to a Protestant audience. The novel represents the influence of American and Mexican culture on such a wedding as a key image of cultural accommodation.

A wedding is one of the most ritualized ceremonies in Mexican custom.[4] Every community has its own special rituals that are expected to be included in the ceremony, and a wedding in the Mexican community always means spending an enormous amount of money and time for a single day's celebration. Ponce's narrative describing the energy and plans that go into an elaborate Mexican wedding is at once hilarious—because of the extremes to which the characters go to complete the traditions of a marriage ceremony— and sad, because an elaborate wedding is all these characters seem to have in their lives. It is bad enough that the characters must exaggerate everything that is characteristic of a Mexican wedding— a large wedding party, a large reception, an elaborate marriage ceremony—but the characters then add the traditions of an American wedding—junior bridesmaids, an outdoor reception. The process of bringing two cultures together can be a disaster as well as a way to deal with contradiction.

While previous examples from *Trini* and *Maravilla* portray successful accommodation of two cultures in individuals and among groups, *The Wedding* is an example of cultural failure. Bringing together two cultures appears as a mix of surfaces with no real understanding of either culture:

> The idea of having a Junior Bridesmaid in her wedding was not something Blanca had thought up. Mostly, it was Lucy who insisted Blanca include a young girl as Junior madrina, just like the Americans. While trying on dresses at La Mas Popular, Lucy had heard a customer ask to see dresses for teenage attendants, or Junior Bridesmaids. Lucy was very impressed. It sounded like a real hep thing! Lucy went to work on Blanca . . . . (73)

This attitude of doing what sounded "hep" identifies most of the characters' understanding of what is done in their community: tradition and "hep" things are equally followed without significant reason or reflection. No character is expected to think for herself or question why something is done. If an idea is traditional—it is adopted; equally, if the idea appears "cool" or "hep"—it is included.

The barrio culture represented in *The Wedding* combines Mexican and American characteristics, integrating them at the material level, but in a superficial way that makes no significant cultural statement. The success of the novel is not dependent upon the introspection of the characters but on convincing a reader that these characters are caught up in a world that completely controls their individual actions.

There are examples of pluralist moments in Lucha Corpi's *Delia's Song*. The Chicano students' group at Berkeley is in the midst of changing the organization's name:

> "What do you think, Delia? Should we become MECHA, Movimiento Estudiantil Chicano de Aztlán?" Julio asked Delia after one of the meetings. "No more MASC [Mexican-American Student Confederation]. No more masks. We are who we are."
> "I'd vote for that," Delia answered. "MECHA. Yes, that sounds good. But, what about the others? Do you think they'll vote it down?" (24)

The students want to declare their unwillingness to assimilate, but the decision is described superficially. This surface accommodation is similar to one in Laura Del Fuego's *Maravilla*. Cece's gang is named Las Belltones; this girls' gang is no different from an Anglo gang (11). In both cases, a name suggests an attempt at cultural pluralism, but the content behind the name is never fully filled in.

III. Revisionism

Unlike the assimilationist and accommodationist, revisionist assumptions about culture include an understanding of cultural norms not as intrinsic, but as constantly under construction. In fact, culture as a term becomes very problematic. No clear and distinguishable characteristics can be identified as specifically belonging to a social group. Culture becomes a relational and dynamic process rather than a stable set of beliefs, values, and representations. There is no possibility of standardization, categorization, or even clear identification of characteristics. The revisionist conception of culture defines the amorphous space created when what was once assumed as clearly identifiable and separate no longer is. In other words, the revisionist conception represents the space beyond dualities, where all experience is allowed and nothing marginalized, a utopian rather than an achieved space. The ideological conception of such a space represents the utopian cultural ideal that Chicana feminists envision. Such a space would allow for female experience to occur without the interference of patriarchy, allow Chicano culture to exist without being marginalized, and would represent an indigenous feminist utopia, which Gloria Anzaldúa calls the "borderland."

Examples of borderland moments are few in these novels but they do exist. Consistently, however, the authors fail to sustain revisionist moments. In *Across the Great River*, Hernández has Doña Anita and Dr. Mendez work together to uncast the evil-eye spell that has been placed upon Kata. Anita does the ritual and Mendez watches her pulse and keeps her warm. Working together, they heal Kata, but the moment is not continued. Mendez immediately breaks into his skepticism: "Yes, I can see the difference in the pulse rate, but I still believe it is because she believes in you as a curer"(113).

Trambley creates such a borderland moment when Trini brings together Tonantzín and the Virgin as I discussed earlier. When Trini declares "I am Tonantzín" and identifies with the melding together of the two worlds, one Christian, and one indigenous, cultural boundaries are temporarily erased (75). The borderland moments appear as glimpses into a new culture of diversity, a "frontera" in the sense of frontier.

Roberta Fernández in *Intaglio* describes a borderland moment and the difficulty in sustaining such a moment. The narrator has been participating in community arts activities:

> For a long time I participated in colorful exhibits in the parks, poetry readings in community centers, sales of folk crafts, coordination of children's folkloric dances. I felt that these activities connected me back to the stimulating creativity of the people who had served as my mentors as I was growing up, at the same time that they satisfied my new needs to move away from an alienating individualism towards a public collectivism much more in keeping with the experiences of my youth. (84)

The narrator is brought up short by her discovery at one particular folk art exhibit of "earrings made to resemble the folk altars"(84). These altars, as Fernández explains, are invested with the deepest spiritual reverence from the community and individuals the narrator has been describing. For the narrator, such "gaudy creations" are devoid of the spiritual respect the community holds for its religious icons. While Nenita can see the artistic value in the altars she remembers as a child and those she sees before her, she is still struck by the shallow understanding the folk artist has for the religious icons. The folk artist defends herself: ". . . I never had any direct contact with the traditional religious sentiment that you are talking about. This is my way of giving tribute to that experience"(85). The narrator buys a pair and is left wondering why she did such a thing.

The coming together of what would appear as two distinct and contradictory cultural values between the respect for religious icons and their artistic value with the so called "tribute" the folk artist claims with her earrings, challenges the narrator to negotiate the borderland moment--when cultures collide. The narrator's response is to include the earrings in her own altar. Thus finding that "They will serve a purpose after all"(86). While taken aback by the insensitivity of the folk artist, the narrator combines the cultural contradiction inherent in the experience and creates a new altar incorporating the gaudy earrings. The moment satisfies the split between two cultures and creates another culture—a borderland culture.

The "borderland" becomes not just a physical place but a state of being. "A border is a dividing line, a narrow strip along a steep edge. A borderland is a vague and undetermined place created by the emotional residue of an unnatural boundary" (Anzaldúa 3). To Anzaldúa an "unnatural boundary" represents the unnaturalness of dualities, representing the ultimate enemy—dualistic thinking. The ability to think and feel without the clear divisions represented in oppositional thinking defines Anzaldúa's new culture:

> So, don't give me your tenets and your laws. Don't give me your lukewarm gods. What I want is an accounting with all three cultures—white, Mexican, Indian. I want the freedom to carve and chisel my own face, to staunch bleeding with ashes, to fashion my own gods out of my entrails. And if going home is denied me then I will have to stand and claim my space, making a new culture—*una cultura mestiza*—with my own lumber, my own bricks and mortar and my own feminist architecture. (22)

For Anzaldúa, traditional Western thought has brought culture to the brink of disaster. By refusing to accept clear distinctions between cultures, by attempting an understanding of difference without marginalization, Anzaldúa imagines communities with new definitions.

Notes

1 Assimilation, as a term and social construct, has lost its usefulness and been replaced with the concepts of acculturation. While assimilation as a social conception is defunct, I still use it as part of the fictional constructions created by literary authors.

2 June Macklin in "'All the good and bad in the world': Women, traditonal medicine, and Mexican American culture" (1980) describes the duality in the nature of a *curandera*:

> As a healer, a woman epitomizes all of the *good* associated with femininity: she is knowledge, self-sacrificing, nurturant, caring, submissive yet protecting, loyal, chaste, and close to divine power; but the same arcane knowledge and ability to traffic with spirits suggests all that is dark, mysterious, and *bad* in the power of being a female. (127)

3 Linda Brown and Kay Mussell explore the relationship between food preparation and consumption to group identity in their work *Ethnic and Regional Foodways in the United States* (1984).

4 For information on marriage and traditions see Edward Murguía, *Chicano Intermarriage: A Theoretical and Empirical Study* (1982); Carlos E. Cortés, ed., *Church Views of the Mexican American* (1974); and Roland G. Tharp, et al., "Changes in Marriage Roles Accompanying the Acculturation of a Mexican-American Wife" (1986).

Chapter III

The Politics of Language

Mexican-American authors must make a decision about whether to represent the dialect of the community from which they come and how they will portray that language. This chapter focuses on language and formal innovation within the narratives, and I argue that they again tend to fall into three categories: those who use traditional standard English; those who employ some bilingualism; and those who write in nonstandard forms of both English and Spanish. A Mexican-American author's relationship to standard English is a political one. Since English represents the dominant culture perhaps more clearly than anything else, the degree to which these authors find standard English adequate to articulate Mexican-American female identity and experience is a measure of their engagement with or opposition to United States cultural norms. A pattern emerges parallel to that described in the previous chapter: the cultural assimilationist uses standard English; the cultural accommodationist uses some bilingualism; and the revisionist disrupts and abandons standard forms.

I. Assimilationism

Across the Great River, a work defined by the publisher as meant for a young adult audience, is again an excellent example of assimilationism in its use of language.[1] Irene Beltrán Hernández chooses to use standard English, although through most of the story no character actually speaks English; the work reads like a "translation." Though the audience is meant to understand the characters are speaking Spanish, but the language itself does not make an appearance.

Reed W. Dasenbrock argues that the "criterion of intelligibility" or accessibility level is normally defined using the standard English reader as norm; hence works that are multi-lingual may be unfairly defined as "unintelligible." Giving examples of works that have been called "unintelligible" because of foreign language us (R. K. Narayan's *The Painter of Signs*, Maxine Hong Kingston's *The Woman Warrior*, Rudolfo Anaya's *Bless Me, Ultima*, and Witi Ihimaera's *Tangi*), Dasenbrock argues that United States mainstream society measures all works against a normative standard English. Hence, a work that uses words or phrases in a language other than English, French, or German and does not translate immediately runs the risk of being called "unintelligible." If French or German appear, the work is considered "sophisticated." The hierarchy is clear: works in standard English are the most natural and normal in American language use; works in standard English that use French or German without translations are "sophisticated"; works that use standard English with foreign words, other than French or German, or terms of the language of popular culture may be accused of being "unintelligible." These Eurocentric assumptions may explain why Beltrán Hernández chooses to use only standard English in her work; the decision, however, represents an assimilationist attitude toward the politics of language.

Exceptions to the use of standard English in *Across the Great River* include only titles not easily translated into English and somewhat familiar to an English speaking audience. "Doña" and "Don" and terms of endearment like "m'ija" are not underlined or given any emphasis to show they come from a language other than English. The words are translated immediately in the text.

> "M'ija, daughter, is there something you would like to take on this trip?" (5)
> As soon as the drops hit his tongue, the man jerks into a sitting position. "Que? What?" (36)

If the author were attempting aural verisimilitude, the work would be in the dialect Spanish spoken at the Mexican/United States border. Instead, it aims for assimilation with the dominant language. The intended audience is one that is literate in standard English and not necessarily in standard Spanish. The possibilities for identification between Kata, the main character, and the readers are thus emphasized and enhanced. Kata's concerns over family responsibility, assigned chores, and playtime represent so-called "universal" childhood interests, limiting cultural difference between Kata and the intended audience. The language difference is then erased by standard English. Important to the assimilationist is the ability to become a part of and identify with the community of choice, and Kata can be identified as a member of that reading community; the one difference that would clearly mark Kata as "other" is not allowed to impede the identification of the reader with the main character.

Sandra Cisneros in *The House on Mango Street* also only uses standard English, with similar exceptions in the use of titles and words that are commonly heard in the United States. The community Cisneros writes about is one that seems to have lost its ability to speak any Spanish and has become mainstreamed into the U. S. culture. Again, the intended audience is young and female, and the narrative attempts to emphasize the similarities between reader and the main character, focusing on a kind of "universalized" young but maturing character, much like Kata in *Across the Great River*.

To these authors, language must not be a barrier between audience and character; however, they do attempt the communication of cultural difference in standard English. Beltrán Hernández's *Across the Great River* describes Anita, the *curandera*:

> Anita finishes rubbing me and makes wide circles with the lemon. It seems she is drawing a giant halo over my entire body, then she takes the lemon and carefully puts it in a glass ashtray that sits on the table near the bed. From her bag she pulls out a box of matches. She strikes one sets the flame under the lemon. The flame seems to want to die out, but Anita holds it firm to the lemon. Soon it seems the lemon begins to breathe, growing larger, then rapidly smaller. My eyes blur as Anita begins to chant under her breath, "Away with you, away to your world," she says, over and over again. (112-13)

The scene described above would rarely occur outside the Spanish speaking community, and Anita would not be chanting in English. Beltrán Hernández might have described the scene in Spanish or had

Anita chant in Spanish, but this would emphasize rather than minimize cultural difference.

Cisneros in *The House on Mango Street* describes a Hispanic world in a northern city where Spanish seems not to function; yet if a reader were actually in those neighborhoods, she would hear Spanish in the streets. The world Cisneros creates does not mirror the language of the community. One story hints that English is probably not the language spoken at home. The main character, Esperanza, is comforting her father:

> Your abuelito is dead, Papa says early one morning in my room. *Está muerto*, and then as if he just heard the news himself, crumples like a coat and cries, my brave Papa cries. I have never seen my Papa cry and don't know what to do. (56)

The reader understands the story from the point of view of Esperanza, who is in fact probably translating everything into English, yet the act of translating itself is muted, never fully represented.

The assumptions about language made in these two works imply that the experience of Mexican-Americans can be articulated in English without necessarily resorting to the use of aural verisimilitude. Even if the "authentic" auditory experience would be in Spanish, the narrators prefer to use the tools of standard English to bridge at the same time they communicate cultural difference. In Beltrán Hernández' and Cisneros' dialogue, moments of difference are played down, mediated, or undercut completely by the use of standard English, "universalizing" the experience for a U. S.-educated reader. Both works are meant for young adult readers, and a reason for the use of standard English may be to avoid challenging the accessibility levels of the intended audience. But the "message" is that standard English is an acceptable vehicle for the representation of the experiences of a Mexican-American community.

Lucha Corpi in *Delia's Song*, a novel intended for a wider audience than young adults, also uses only standard English and accepted formal innovation to tell her story. Writing in a modified stream-of-consciousnes technique used by authors like Virginia Woolf, James Joyce, and William Faulkner, it is clear that Corpi has been heavily influenced by modernist fiction. Corpi translates all experience into English, but allows one of her characters to acknowledge the translating, representing and then erasing the linguistic gap:

> She [Delia] began telling it in Spanish, which she always spoke with her aunt, but as she related the episode about her near-accident and her fear of being mad, she switched to English, something that Marta found very amusing and interesting but not strange, as she herself would on occasion do the same thing. "There are things," she had told Cloti many times, "that one can only express in mother's language." (99)

While the characters may express a need to speak in Spanish, the narrative does not often acknowledge such a need. In fact, despite Marta's statement here, no experience in the novel seems to necessitate expression in anything other than English.

Like Cisneros, Corpi uses Spanish only once and also to describe a scene with Delia's parents. The Spanish is italicized and clearly marked in the standard form for a foreign language. This is the only time in the novel that Corpi practices code-switching, representing it in standard written form emphasizing the distinction between Spanish and English: "'*Sí, m'ija*,' her mother said, not paying much attention. . . . '*Trajiste tu* report card' her father asked Delia, . . ."(57).[2] This is standard form for writing spoken foreign language. Corpi uses standard Spanish here and does not distinguish an accent in either language nor any experimentation to distinguish English from Spanish.

Cisneros, Beltrán Hernández, and Corpi have in common an interest in depicting cultural difference which is subordinated to their interest in "universal" experience. In standard English, cultural difference becomes less alienating to a U. S. audience. A mimetic representation of dialect would require different assumptions about "universal" experience which is not part of the agendas of these authors.

II. Accommodationism

Among the novels in this category, language variations predominate. No longer solely occupied with expressing Mexican-American experience in standard English, some authors begin the process of disrupting traditional forms of language. The accommodationist conception of language assumes that standard forms of English do not provide adequate aural verisimilitude in representations of the Mexican-American community; that standard forms can be manipulated so a reader can get a sense of an authentic auditory experience; and that standard forms of English and Spanish can be placed in the same sentence, as bilingualism.[3]   The accommodationist uses standard forms of *both* languages in order to get a more accurate understanding of Mexican-American aural experiences; with only some minor adjustments in standard forms of English and Spanish, the written form can represent more closely Mexican-American aural experience.   Code-switching becomes acceptable and frequent.   Important in code-switching is the acknowledgement that one is using a foreign language, assigning value to two languages, separate and distinct, but brought together in one sentence.   Hence, one language, usually Spanish, is marked as the "foreign" language by being italicized or appearing in quotes. English and Spanish are still two separate and distinct languages, but they can be used in the same prose work as long as the traditional distinct standard forms of each language are maintained.   As Gloria T. Hull in *Reading Literature by U.S. Third World Women* (1984) puts it:

> Awareness of bilingualism as an issue is particularly apparent in the Hispanic work in which both English and Spanish are seen by authors as viable alternatives.   Reinforcing new feelings of identification and pride, Hispanic women writers routinely combine the two languages—or deliberately choose Spanish over English.   Their doing so forces a non-Spanish-speaking reader, especially if she/he is also English mono-lingual, to think about language, cultural chauvinism, and linguistic outreach, and to confront within him/ herself whatever emotions result from not being catered to, from being cast into the position of an outsider.   (5)

Laura del Fuego in *Maravilla*, Estela Portillo Trambley in *Trini*, and Mary Helen Ponce in *The Wedding*, use code-switching in order to represent their characters' experiences.   Portillo Trambley uses standard Spanish sparingly and does not experiment with nonstandard forms of language even in dialogue; hence, aural verisimilitude itself is not a priority in the novel.   In the following conversation taking place in Mexico among Mexicans, English is almost completely substituted for the Spanish in which the conversation would actually occur:

"Well, my date got drunk, and I was late getting home. Papá was waiting. !Ay, ay, ay, Dios mío!" the girl laughed as her hands played skillfully in the air. "Papá was at the door with his gun! He put it right to Lalo's temple and told him to scat. Poor Lalo! He didn't even feel the gun! He opened one eye, looked at Papá, smiled and left. Just like that!" (137)

The only Spanish that Portillo Trambley does not translate is "Dios mío."

Earlier in the novel, Portillo Trambley atypically includes a Spanish song which is not fully translated.

"El piojo y la pulga
Se van a casar
Les pregunta el cura
Si saben rezar . . .
Todito sabemos
Y nada sin falta
Contesta el raton de su ratonal . . .
Que haga la boda
Yo pondre el maiz . . ." (49)

She is very careful to make sure that the non-Spanish reader has at least some idea as to what the song is about: "'Do you know the marriage of the fleas?' 'El piojo y la pulpa.' Tonio grinned" (48). By calling the song "all nonsense," she undercuts the importance of a literal understanding or a full translation of the song. Eliud Martínez in "Personal Vision in the Short Stories of Estela Portillo Trambley" (1985) describes Portillo Trambley's skill with standard English:

"I like to say," Portillo Trambley has told us, "whee, look at me, look at the beautiful words." These . . . show that Portillo Trambley is a writer who venerates language both for its own sake and because of its powers to dramatize ordinary phenomena . . . . Her language is eloquent, sometimes exquisite, and always correct. . . . One finds very few contractions in her writings and only a sprinkling of Spanish words, which she does not force. (74)

Martínez sees Portillo Trambley's work as belonging to traditional and formal standards of English style, and yet willing to use a few words of Spanish.

Like the assimilationist model, a more accommodationist one depends on a clear distinction between one language and the other. But, at the same time, the willingness to put two languages together in the same sentence marks a difference between the accommodationist and the assimilationist. So while Portillo Trambley uses very little Spanish, she is still willing to take the standard forms of English and Spanish and bring them together. This represents a very limited form of code-switching, which I call Spanish code-switching because the bulk of the prose is in English, and Spanish is still very much "other."

In *Maravilla*, Laura del Fuego also uses Spanish code-switching, but she accomplishes limited aural verisimilitude by using both standard Spanish and nonstandard forms. The nonstandard Spanish includes the slang of East Los Angeles teenagers of the 1960s. The novel describes poor working-class Mexican-Americans in the barrio. Del Fuego is concerned with representing authentically the language spoken in these communities where actual code-switching is a very common occurrance in dialogue. Unlike the previous novels, and with the exception of Cisneros' *The House on Mango Street* where a barrio community is implied but not explicit, the narrative action in this novel occurs in a clearly identified Mexican-American community. There is a greater attempt at giving written form to the auditory experience of the neighborhood. Del Fuego communicates a clear difference, however, between the language spoken in the community and the standard written representation of it.

For del Fuego and unlike Cisneros, depicting the actual language of the community is part of the narrative. The rules that govern standard written English allow for the experience to be communicated well enough that del Fuego does not feel compelled to explore nonstandard written forms. She simply inserts the Spanish, specifying it as a foreign language by italicization. Code-switching only in dialogue or when attempting to record a character's thoughts, del Fuego marks the Spanish "foreign" and records these characters' accents that would be heard in the pronunciation of English by changing the orthography of those words:

> "You maum?"
> I realized that she hadn't understood, so I said, *"Mi madre."*
> *"Ah si, su madre,"* she said reverently.
> "I hate her! She's a witch."
> *"Ay, Dios, Santito!"* she gasped.

"What's wrong?"
"Ess thess Sail-em, seventeen cent-oory?"
"What are you talking about?"   (6)

The dialogue is depicted with contractions and incomplete sentences.
Spanish is not always limited to a few words mixed in with English
but whole sentences in dialogue: "'Consuelo, but everyone calls me
Cece.' '*Su nombre es muy hermosa*'" (7).[4] Del Fuego's verisimilitude
requires decisions about how to represent aural experience in
standard forms. By modifying dialogue and not abandoning standard
English in the prose, del Fuego can represent the spoken form in
Spanish code-switching and keep the accessibility level high. This
compromise between dialogue and prose exposition is characteristic
of accommodationists.

Roberta Fernández in *Intaglio* uses standard forms of Spanish
and English in her work, even going so far as to provide a glossary of
some of the Spanish terms used in the text. Clearly for Fernández
keeping the text accessible to an English reading audience is important.
While attempting to represent the culture accurately, representing
the aural experience is not a priority for Fernández.   She
accommodates written Spanish within standard written English.

For Mary Helen Ponce in *The Wedding*, standard forms of
written English are not enough to express experience accurately.
The characteristics that stand out in this work are the altered spelling,
a written representation of the sound of accents in characters' voices,
and the use of slang terms of the period; she also uses nonstandard
spelling of English words and nonstandard grammar in dialogue.
The Wedding is a novel about the marriage between a girl from the
Los Angeles barrio and her boyfriend from the barrio gangs of the
1950s. Ponce includes the popular English and Spanish words of the
period, words like "cool" and "ese." Making no distinction between
English slang and Spanish slang, Ponce does not italicize words in the
novel: "'That guy ain't got no class, esa! How come he ain't askin ya
to the Zenda?'" (20).

Like del Fuego, Ponce is interested in creating a verbal
exchange that includes the accent of the speakers.[5] Since no standards
exist for novelists creating accents in dialogue, an author must create
her own rules. Ponce deviates from standard forms in dialogue or in
representing internal thoughts; for example, "all right" becomes "all

reet," "show" becomes "chow," "chairs" becomes "shairs," and "to" becomes "ta." The use of deviant spelling provides the reader with an experience of the nonstandard English of the neighborhood.

Ponce, del Fuego, Beltrán Fernández and Trambley all imply that standard English is not the language of the characters they have created but is appropriate for the omniscient narration of Mexican-American experience. One difference between the language of standard-English readers and that of the characters in the novels is represented by the code-switching into Spanish, the altered spelling, and the nonstandard grammar accentuating "difference." These three authors, unlike Corpi, Cisneros, and Beltrán Hernández, insist that the experience they are trying to communicate requires adjusting standard forms of language. Each author has either deviated from the standard or, as Portillo Trambley has done, put two standard forms of language together. The nonstandard forms that accommodationists use do not significantly impede accessibility for a standard-English reading audience; an unfamiliarity with Spanish would not hinder an understanding of these novels, since most of it is usually immediately translated by the authors within the context of the dialogue. While some of the Spanish, especially in del Fuego's work, would be interruptive to a reader unfamiliar with the language, the narrative is not dependent upon an understanding of Spanish. While both assimilationists and accommodationists acknowledge two distinct languages, Spanish and English, the assimilationists generally will not mix the two languages together; the accommodationists does combine them.

III. Revisionism

Denise Chávez in *Last of the Menu Girls* and Margarita Cota-Cárdenas in *Puppet* (1985) find standard English an inadequate vehicle for their narratives. The revisionist conception of language does not assume that there are two distinct languages being used by the Chicano community. For the revisionist, a new language has emerged from the mingling of Spanish, English, and the languages of indigenous populations of north and central America. Gloria Anzaldúa calls this language a border tongue and not just because people living near the Mexican/United States border speak it. In *Borderlands/La Frontera*, Anzaldúa argues that a new language has emerged that is capable of articulating the experience of cultures in conflict:

> For people who are neither Spanish nor live in a country in which Spanish is the first language; for a people who live in a country in which English is the reigning tongue but who are not Anglo; for a people who cannot entirely identify with either standard (formal, Castillian) Spanish nor standard English, what recourse is left to them but to create their own language? A language which they can connect their identity to, one capable of communicating the realities and values true to themselves—a language with terms that are neither *espoñal ni inglés*, but both. We speak a patois, a forked tongue, a variation of two languages. (55)

Later, Anzaldúa includes the languages of the indigenous populations in this "patois," and *Borderlands/La Frontera*, as its title suggests, is *written* in this new language:

> On December 2nd when my sun goes into my first house, I celebrate *el dia de la Chicana y el Chicano*. On that day I clean my altars, light my *Coatlalopeuh* candle, burn sage and copal, take *el bano para espantar basura*, sweep my house. (88)

The first assumption made by the revisionist is that neither English nor Spanish is a distinctly different language in the Chicano community. A third language has emerged, a language with its own distinct regional variations, slang terms, and regional accents. Anzaldúa provides a list of the languages spoken by the border inhabitant:

1. Standard English
2. Working class and slang English
3. Standard Spanish
4. Standard Mexican Spanish
5. North Mexican Spanish dialect
6. Chicano Spanish (Texas, New Mexico, Arizona and California have regional variations)
7. Tex-Mex
8. *Pachuco* (called caló) (55)

The very concept of "standard" forms of language is directly challenged by this third language, spoken in unassimilated Mexican-American communities, a language specific to each community.

Denise Chávez in *The Last of the Menu Girls* provides a clear example of how this third language can be written. Chávez refuses to acknowledge the "foreignness" of Spanish. The novel takes place in urban New Mexico where the main character, Rocío, is maturing and creating her identity. Depicting how a young Chicana develops as a writer, Chávez is very interested in describing the forces that contribute to an individual's growth. For most of the novel, Spanish is rarely used. In fact, standard English is the prose vehicle throughout the novel until the final chapter. Initially the novel appears to represent many of the assumptions of the assimilationist, until the final story. The language code-switches into Spanish except that it is not marked any differently from English; there are no italicized words, no quotes, nothing highlighted to give a reader a hint that both English and Spanish are included in the prose. The languages are combined "naturally":

> ¡Ay, estas hierbas malditas! Mi comadre will come and take me home. I'll come back tomorrow and finish the work. Maybe I can get some of the chamacos to come and help me pull these weeds. I guess I'm getting old. They need the money, esos chamacos flojos! They can come to la comadre's and I'll tell them what to do. (184)

The interweaving and mixing of the two languages in the creation of one new language represents for Chávez the language understood by Rocío's community in New Mexico. The "new" language is similar to the one first articulated in *Cuentos: Stories by Latinas* (1983) edited by Alma Gómez, Cherríe Moraga, and Mariana Romo-Carmona. The editors believe "the issues of bilingualism and bi-culturalism are crucial" (x) and take a revisionist position which is becoming increasingly important in Chicana fiction:

> *Cuentos* validates the use of "spanglish" and "tex-mex." Mixing English and Spanish in our writing and talking is a legitimate and creative response to acculturation. It doesn't mean that we are illiterate or assimilated as we are sometimes labeled by the anglo and Latin American elite. (x-xi)

They continue the discussion in a footnote, explaining their use of Spanish for a "bi-cultural reader" and Latina in the United States:

> For this reason we have only translated Spanish references in works written predominantly in English and where the references are critical to

understanding the work. We have not italicized the Spanish or footnoted the translations in order to have the text visually reflect the bi-cultural experience. (xi)

While Chávez provides a new way to write the language of the border community, Margarita Cota-Cárdenas in *Puppet* takes the most radical approach to expressing the aural experience of a Chicano community. Mostly written in nonstandard Spanish, Cota-Cárdenas' novel switches into English occasionally. The punctuation is nonstandard, pauses in the narration and dialogue are represented by elipses, and dialogue is not marked by quotation marks:

BRIIIIIINNNNNG...Hello? Quién...Is that you Memo?

--Hi Petra? Yeah, it's Memo...Pues, te llamaba pa' decirte que, pues que mataron...

--Memo, what did you say? Qué quién mató a quién?

--...a Puppet. Mataron a Puppet.

--Cuándo, Memo? Cómo? How can that be? My God!.!

--...La policía. Jue anoche, la Policía lo mató anoche...lo balacearon. No lo vites en las news? (1)

Cota-Cárdenas has combined and changed standard forms of writing to create a written language that represents the aural experience specific to San Antonio, Texas. Much of the Spanish is the vernacular spoken in central Texas and not Castillian Spanish. Cota-Cárdenas does the same to English. Obvious, of course, are the variations on standard punctuation, but even more deliberate are the language shifts from Spanish to English without any warning to a reader:

—Okay, okay, ma! Don't get so self-righteous, anyway...I just felt dumb not knowing what they were talking about...No, me tratan muy bien, well you know a couple of them are my close friends...Me dejan hablar lo que quiera en español, allí en el trabajo... (8)

In this excerpt, the speaker is a woman who speaks mostly English and knows Spanish but does not speak *standard* Spanish. Most of the other characters speak Spanish, and those who speak mostly

English are recognized by their constant code-switching.

A reader unfamiliar with Spanish will find this novel inaccessible; it would be "unintelligible" to a standard English reader. *Puppet* requires work from a reader, even one who reads in Spanish because of the heavy use of local dialect. She must first become familiar with the variant punctuation and English code-switching before the reading becomes smoother. In the altered punctuation, bold print, capitalized words, and code-switching into English, Cota-Cárdenas is challenging standard written forms and the reader's ability to keep up. The experience narrated in the novel includes the experience of reading the novel. By challenging the reader, creating another form, Cota-Cárdenas claims the community's experience of Puppet's death requires its own language. The language Cota-Cárdenas portrays does not necessarily mirror the actual lived experience, but it does come considerably closer to mimetic accuracy than Beltrán Hernández' translated English in *Across the Great River*.

The revisionist conception of language acknowledges that the Chicano experience is different from that of the Anglo culture. The revisionist seeks to exemplify and to articulate that "difference," and standard forms of language serve to undercut or minimize difference. The language of the partially assimilated Chicano community, for the revisionist, must be recorded and not translated into standard English, becoming part of the identity of the Chicano community. The language of the "new mestiza" begins the process of identifying a community, and the revisionist comes closer to a radical understanding of the Chicano community. Does the revisionist conception of language also have something to offer in terms of an understanding of gender? That question will be explored in the next chapter.

Notes

1   Included on the back jacket of the book is the following blurb from the publisher: "*Across the Great River* is recommended reading for young adults, as well as mature readers."

2   To code-switch, the sentence has a word or phrase used that is not of that same language, for example, "the brain" becomes "*la* brain" or the phrase "you see" becomes "*tu vease*" in an otherwise English sentence.

3   For a broader understanding of bilingualism at an introductory level, the following article is especially useful: Guadalupe Valdés, "The Language Situation of Mexican Americans" (1988). Important in Valdés' discussion is the concept of diglossia:
     A situation known as "diglossia" is said to exist when two languages in a bilingual community take on specialized and complementary functions, so that the first language is used primarily for the home-related spheres of activity, while the second is used for all formal, institutional, and official matters. (114)
For more information on biligualism, see: Heinz Kloss, *The American Bilingual Tradition* (1977); Sandra L. McKay and Sau-ling Cynthia Wong, eds., *Language and Diversity: Problem or Resource?* (1988); Hugo Baetens Beardsmore, *Bilingualism: Basic Principles* (1986); Kenji Hajuta, *Mirror of Language: The Debate on Bilingualism* (1986); and Rosaura Sánchez, *Chicano Discourse: Socio-Historic Perspectives* (1983).

4   The use of non-standard *hermosa* instead of the standard Spanish *hermoso* represents the challenge authors make to standard forms of language. Many Mexican-American authors experiment with non-standard language forms in order to attempt a more accurate aural representation of the vernacular.

5   Raymond Chapman focuses on the different written forms authors use in order to represent dialect in "The Reader as Listener: Dialect and Relationships in *The Mayor of Casterbridge*" (1989). He states that the representation of speech by an author is usually a stylistic characteristic. Since no standards exist for novelists creating accents in dialogue, an author must create her own rules. One of the most common is altered orthography as Chapman notes:
     Once a system of orthography has been established in a language, it is not difficult to give some impression of dialect in writing. If normal spelling is used for narrative and for unmarked speech, deviant spelling readily

shows deviant pronunciation. Indeed, the effect may be greater than that of dialect heard in real speech, which would be scarcely noticed in many situations if the message were clearly conveyed. (165)

Chapter IV

The Politics of Gender

I seek our woman's face, our true features, the positive and the negative seen clearly, free of the tainted biases of male dominance. I seek new images of identity, new beliefs about ourselves, our humanity and worth no longer in question. (Anzaldúa 87)

Calling for a new identity, a feminist Chicana identity, free of "male dominance," Anzaldúa seeks new representations of "woman." Among contemporary women writers, Anzaldúa is not alone, yet there are also those who do not wish to abandon traditional gender roles and patterns of society. For some of them, issues of gender are not as central as are issues of relationships between races and among dominant cultures and subcultures and issues of class. Gender becomes muted in such works, but the authors who do demand issues of gender be addressed are creating a new vision that subverts and abandons prescribed roles for women and men. Those authors are exploring the consciousness of the "new mestiza." Each of the three phases Elaine Showalter describes can be applied, with some cultural adjustments, to the analysis of works by contemporary Mexican-American women novelists.

I. The Feminine Phase

The first phase, the feminine phase as described by Showalter, involves "internalized . . . assumptions about female nature" as defined by patriarchy. Translated cross-culturally, this involves for Mexican-American writers creating female characters whose identities are grounded in traditional gender roles and characterized by a preoccupation with the needs of others, especially male members of the family. Consequently, this "feminine phase" corresponds in many ways with the assimilationist conception of culture, which functions by internalizing assumptions that belong to the dominant culture. In the feminine phase, one internalizes the culture's assumptions for femininity and masculinity. The gender issue, hence, has its equivalent in the broader cultural construct.

This feminine phase is actually where most of the novels under discussion begin. While the majority of the novels move from initial description of gender stereotypes, and some vacillate between the feminine and female phases, one work, Beltrán Hernández' *Across the Great River*, best articulates the appropriateness of conventional gendered roles; her novel is representative of the feminine phase.

In *Across the Great River* Beltrán Hernández' creates in her main character, Kata, a child becoming inducted into the roles and responsibilities of a Mexican woman. These include a serious preoccupation with the needs of the male members of the family. As I indicated earlier, the story of this family's illegal border crossing is told from the point-of-view of Kata, a ten-year-old girl. This child's perspective involves an understanding of the expectations of her as a female family member. The "indoctrination," I would call it, into womanhood described by Kata is her personal experience representing the internalization of a culture's accepted roles for women.

Beltrán Hernández' novel deals with many different themes, such as coming-of-age, the relationship of the female to *familia*, interpersonal relationships between the generations, and authority. Though all of these involve significant gender differences, the relationship of the female to *familia* best exemplifies the representation of gender in this novel. The first few pages of the novel set up a traditional hierarchical family structure, with the father as absolute authority. In order to give Kata her own story, however, Beltrán Hernández creates a situation so that Kata can assume the responsibilities of the head of the family by separating Kata's father from the family and seriously injuring her mother. The active members left in the family are Kata and her baby brother who, if the boy had been older, would have assumed authority. By removing the parents, Beltrán Hernández allows Kata a more active role than the traditional passive one expected of a Mexican female daughter and bestows on her a socially "legitimate" amount of autonomy. Kata still remains traditionally feminine, however, because her authority is socially sanctioned by the male culture and is exercised only for a finite period of time, in an emergency. Once her parents return, Kata will resume her role as an obedient traditional Mexican daughter.

While the story of Kata could have led to an undercutting of traditional Mexican values, Beltrán Hernández does not make that choice. The ideological position in the novel assumes the legitimacy of patriarchy, and most of the characters seek to reinforce it. Even a character like Doña Anita, who as a traditional healer is a woman of some autonomy and authority, does not question the assumption of male authority; instead she seeks the re-establishment of the male as head of Kata's family.

Kata can recognize easily what is appropriate for a woman and what is not. Those women who do things that are culturally inappropriate are evil women, as is the wife of the local doctor. Kata describes Pilar Mendez: "She pulls out a cigarette and lights it. I gasp in horror, for Mexican women do not smoke in the presence of others" (96). Given Kata's experience as a traditionally raised Mexican child, cigarette smoking is an instant signal to Kata that she is in the presence of an evil woman; inappropriate gender behavior is a sign of moral failure. Because Pilar does not follow appropriate norms of behavior, she is constructed as a villain, who causes Kata to have nightmares. Indeed, Doña Anita is fairly certain that Pilar is the person who has cast the evil eye on Kata. As the local *curandera*, Doña Anita must perform a ceremony in order to rid Kata of the evil cast upon her, a ritualized expulsion of non-feminine behavior from the community.

In this novel, to respect the traditional ways is automatically good and to go against them is automatically bad. Because the border crossing was illegal, the family must return to Mexico in the end in order to reaffirm traditional understandings of right and wrong. It is the women who must constantly remind authority figures, the males, of the inherent superiority of tradition, as Doña Anita does: "A man's dreams are always different from a woman's because they think of themselves first, then they think of the needs of the family" (31).

Kata's mother articulates her belief in the inherent goodness of the past: "Mama answers just as cautiously, 'It's just that we are so unfamiliar with the American ways and customs. In Mexico, our village life was so simple and happier'" (123). Doña Anita's character, of course, represents the traditional past and the need to acknowledge its rightful place in the modern world. Doña Anita speaks with "feminine" authority, contingent upon her support of the traditional past and her nurturing skills.

The end of the story represents the ideological position articulated by the events in the novel: the reestablishment of the authority of the father. Doña Anita is able to get Kata's father out of jail and returned to his rightful place as head of the family. Doña Anita is the force that keeps traditional authority from losing power among the community. Very little has changed in terms of the underlying power structure in place at the beginning of the novel. Based upon the assumptions of the Mexican culture and the experiences Kata's father has survived, he is now ready to take a more appropriate authority position in his family. It is this authority that Kata learns and relates, thus retelling the story of patriarchy. At the end of the novel, a reunited and wealthier family is back in Mexico, replicating the central myth of the immigrant from Mexico: the dream of being able to return rich to the beloved Mexican country.

The gender role that Kata is assigned at the beginning of the novel, interrupted during the adventurous river crossing, has only been re-enforced at the end: the traditional role of the woman, which is to support the male and the family unit, has remained constant throughout the novel. Kata describes it for us:

> I get up to follow her [Kata's mother], but Anita's hand holds me back.
> "Wait, Kata. She's all right."
> I turn to grandfather who smiles down at me. I have no choice but to wait until they consent for me to follow. (133)

Kata turns to the eldest male for "permission" even to accompany her mother. Conventional gender arrangements are not challenged.

Estela Portillo Trambley's *Trini* contains a similar reverence and respect for tradition. In the traditions of the tribe, a woman's role appears to be the same as in modern Mexico: service to the family with the male as ultimate authority; however, the Tarahumara culture is presented in this novel as a benign force in relationship to women and not destructive, as the present Mexican culture is. As Trini grows up and takes on the duties of hearth keeper for the family and as female role model for her younger sister, the narrator describes a romanticized and idyllic world. When Trini's devout

Catholic aunt arrives to take on the responsibilities of senior female, the benign relationship between the girls and their culture is shattered. A more stringent hierarchical relationship between family members is established and the idyllic childhood is lost. Trini learns that the ultimate responsibility of a family member is complete allegiance to that family, a truth she is never released from.

Accepting assigned gender roles becomes a personal odyssey for Trini. Once the family moves to a city in Mexico, Trini is introduced to the drudgery of life in a city as doubly oppressed, both woman and indigenous. The goal, for Trini, becomes a return to the idyllic (and romanticized) valley of her childhood.

Trini, in part the personalized history of the Mexican-American culture and its movement northward, is a larger mythic story represented by the personal narrative of one woman. From her first dawning awareness as a child of her gender-assigned role to her flight from her husband in order to give her children a more secure existence, to her realization that even after she has achieved her goal of land, Trini's awareness of her gender role never progresses out of the feminine phase. After meeting all her material needs, Trini is left searching for something more in the final pages. Unhappy and lonely and still in search of that idyllic valley, Trini is empty. Tonio, her husband, does not love her, nor does she love him. The novel concludes with Trini's longing for her true love, Sabochi, the father of her second child. Trini decides to tell her son of his real father, "the ahua of Cusihuiriachi" (171), and promises to take him to meet his father. Sabochi is the leader of a desert village whose inhabitants continue to live an indigenous existence without modern conveniences. To Trini, returning her son to his indigenous past represents her continued search for the idyllic valley. If she cannot have her valley, maybe her son can. Trini understands her other children, Tonio's children, could never return to such a past; they want the televisions and cars of modern society. The same things their father craves.

Bringing father and son together represents her new dream. She remains nurturer and restorer of a man's family. Trini began her life as a member of an indigenous tribe. The death of her mother, the arrival of her Catholic aunt, the indoctrination into mainstream Mexican society shattered that idyllic life. Trini's limited assimilation into United States mainstream culture only leads to further alienation. Returning to the past is represented in the novel as a positive response to modern existence, a reclaiming of cultural and racial identity. Trini's gender role, however, has only deepened at the end of the novel. Her duty continues to be to men and their children.

In "The Female Hero in Chicano Literature," Carmen Salazar Parr and Genevieve M. Ramírez argue that the "female hero . . . will exemplify those traits generally associated with the male literary hero" (47). They trace this "hero" in the character of Trini and also define her dream: "What she seeks is the ideal circumstance in which she had seen her mother: land, a home, and her family united and supported by a hardworking, faithful, and loving husband" (57). Salazar Parr and Ramírez are accurate in their interpretation of Tini's goal: a return to the pre-lapserian valley. Their conclusion, however, about Trini is more problematic:

> She appears through most of the novel as an unreal figure, the caring mother, the forgiving victim of male-inflicted abuses. Nevertheless, at the close of the novel she finally rejects Tonio because of his betrayals of her; no longer the idealized symbol of selflessness, she is now a human being who will not tolerate what must rightfully be rejected or avenged. (59)

But it is not in character for Trini to be intolerant; she has endured throughout all the novel. She is actually recreating her original dream, only this time without Tonio: "Faintly, like the moonlight filtering through trees, the flicker of a new dream was born, a strange and splendid thing to build upon, a new adventure" (245). By taking her son to his true father and "recapturing . . . something that had been lost with her husband," Trini is simply seeking the ideal she has always had of her mother's life and one she did not find with Tonio (245). The only real rejection is of modern society which is the culmination of its own mythical origins. Portillo Trambley has come full circle. By bringing Trini back to her original search for the idyllic valley, Trini may begin a new myth and possibly a new society. Whatever Portillo Trambley's intentions may be, they are not specified in the text. The end of the novel has Trini contemplating an attempt to simply introduce her son to his biological father.

II. The Female Phase

Patriarchy has among its many characteristics specific prescriptions and definitions for femininity, and ethnic cultures in the United States are no more immune to societal assumptions for gender roles than is the dominant culture, though they may function somewhat differently. As noted, Showalter defines the feminist phase, which I call the female phase, as a point when "women are historically enabled to reject the accommodating postures of femininity and to use literature to dramatize the ordeal of wronged womanhood" (138). This phase is a critical exploration of traditional gender roles. These authors attempt to accommodate tensions which are inevitable when the social demands on a female character are in direct conflict with her individual needs.

The critique of gender roles can be seen in a detailed reading of Ponce's *The Wedding*. Her characters have no conscious conception of their political situation in a larger cultural environment. They are male gang members of an East L. A. barrio, female groupies of that gang, and community members of the turf occupied by "Los Tacones." Ponce's novel is a description of the one event looked forward to by these characters—the wedding between Blanca and Cricket, Los Tacones' gang leader. While the characters are not aware of the fact that they are victims of a limited education and have experienced indoctrination into prescribed gender roles and accepted forms of behavior that negate their opportunity to function beyond the neighborhood community, the reader recognizes the satirical and ironic position in Ponce's authorial undercutting of the characters' limited awareness. In many ways, *The Wedding* is a comedy of Mexican-American manners. Tey Diana Rebolledo, in "Walking the Thin Line: Humor in Chicana Literature," acknowledges the importance of humor emerging in Chicana works as part of their critique of patriarchy:

A criticism of the Mexican-American system or of sexism itself by women is, in effect, a breaking of the ranks of ethnic solidarity and an abandonment of "the culture." Thus, the system creates tremendous pressures and feelings of ambivalence for the writer, feelings which she sometimes expresses directly and sometimes expresses indirectly through humor and irony. (95)

For Ponce, humor and irony are her weapons in her assault on and indictment of assigned gender roles in both cultures, the ethnic and the dominant one, and she carefully identifies the culprits for the barrio's ills as poverty, ignorance, racism, the internalization of assigned gender roles, and social neglect. This combination of social ills has created a world that destroys any possibility of changing ingrained patterns. A woman can only look forward to a nice wedding and her responsibilities as a traditional wife. Blanca, the main character, can consciously envision only one moment of happiness: her wedding day. It is this very narrow world for women that the narrative critiques in order "to dramatize the ordeal of wronged womanhood" as Showalter has characterized it. While Ponce's novel may be describing the barrio of the 1950s, the narrative is also implying how very little things have changed, indeed, how they may have worsened for women.

Blanca's world is represented by the preoccupations of an eighteen-year-old, Mexican-American, heterosexual woman living in the barrio. Her mind is occupied with boys, a longing for a "cool dude" boyfriend who drives a classy car and has a decent or "clean" job. Working in the fields as a migrant picker is not considered a clean job. In order to get the desired boyfriend, Blanca must be a "cool chick." The prescription for being a cool chick includes the following: "She plastered her face with Max Factor pancake makeup, lots of Maybelline and Tangee Real Hot Red lipstick, then rolled her pompadour higher than usual" (6). Putting on high heels, Blanca is preparing for a dance, one of the few pleasures she has in her life. The brand names Ponce includes for the makeup, for example, represent the skewed manner in which the commodities of the dominant culture invade the barrio culture. Its other cultural forms, specifically films and music, are also identified and integrated into the community.

Buying cheap, name brand U. S. products contributes to the parodying of the popular culture of the American teen world: ducktail hairdos for the boys and pompadours or bee hives for the girls. Ponce, however, takes this teen world and shows the extravagant form it takes in a blue-collar Mexican-American community of zoot-suiters. The young adult world of the barrio is littered with low-rider Chevys and Fords, Lucky Strike cigarettes, super high high-heels, and tailor-made suits for poverty stricken gang members who end up in debt for the "cool drapes" look. The teens believe in a superficial world in order to give substance to an otherwise insubstantial and empty existence.

The community is ill educated. "Like most of her friends, Blanca had attended school only to the eighth grade" (10). "She would tell herself, I'm too dumb. All I know is 2 and 2 are 4, Columbus discovered America, and how to pick fruit" (10). She was never encouraged to work at her studies by her family, her peers, or her teachers. The message from the neighborhood was clear: education is not important. Getting a job is important. The same message comes from the dominant culture as well.

Blanca, without skills, finds she has little to offer a world outside the barrio, which rejects her through condescension or outright racism. Blanca knows the inhospitable response she will meet outside her community and "feared having to leave the barrio" (13). Her only place of available employment is "los turkeys," a poultry farm where Blanca plucks feathers off turkeys. This is considered a good job by the barrio community, which considers anything not in the heat of the fields a good job.

The only positive experience Blanca receives from this job is the opportunity for comraderie among the women workers, mostly other Mexican-Americans. The comraderie involves a community of women who represent Blanca's future: "Most of them had children. All worked to help pay rent, buy food and clothes and to now and then pay a bail bondsman or lawyer to free a husband or son from jail" (15-16). These are the factory workers whose reason for working outside the house is that the male head of the household does not earn enough, is out of work, or is not part of the family. In the barrio, a woman must work outside the home, even though it is also assumed she should be at home taking care of hearth and children; a woman who does both things is not respected for either. The material necessity to work outside the home does not replace the stigma that comes with it. When these women were younger and responsible only for themselves, they worked and lived for shopping. Once married, however, they work for the financial survival of the family.

For Blanca, the job at the poultry farm gives her financial independence from her mother. She is willing to contribute to her own room and board, but beyond those expenditures, her money is hers to spend as she pleases, especially because there is no parental authority to challenge her.

> Being single sure is the life, Blanca often thought. I can do what I wants, go where I wanna go and ain't nobody gots nuthin to say about it. Her mother rarely asked where she was going nor what time she would return. Since her father had died years before, Blanca was under no obligation to explain her whereabouts to a male relative. (17)

This obligation-free life is unusual. The fact that Blanca has no male relatives to whom she must answer is rare; most of the other female characters in the novel have some male they must obey. Blanca is considered very lucky by her peer group because she is not responsible to anyone, whether male or female. By allowing Blanca this degree of autonomy, the narrative can explore other issues that entrap women in stagnant roles. Instead of Blanca's being entrapped by a father or elder male family member, Ponce's character is influenced by community and cultural codes. Ponce locates the oppression in ideology and not in individual male characters.

Ponce creates a character, then, whose values are formed not by her immediate family but by her community of peers. She is a product of the neighborhood and hence has little if any direction in her life that is not totally defined by her community. In fact, the novel is most concerned with the influence of "the streets" on the individual. The community is represented by the gangs, the popular culture that makes its way into the neighborhood, the female peer group, and the need to be accepted by the standards of a youth community. This absolute "freedom" is short lived. Once Blanca marries Cricket, the mundane responsibilities of married life (husband, household, and children) will settle around her; Blanca is already pregnant by the time she marries. Until she marries, Blanca is free to do as she wishes, but, of course, "as she wishes" is what the community has told her she wishes. She can dream only a limited dream:

> She plucked away, humming softly to herself, assured this job would enable her to have a nice wedding. I'll be the first in my family to get married in the church, she gloated. I'm gonna make my mama so happy! And Lucy so jealous! Gosh! I never did gets to high school, but I'm gonna have me a big

wedding. I'll show'm. . . . Blanca's round face paled at the thought of so much happiness! (17-18)

Ponce's strategy is to undercut Blanca's perception of happiness and show the actual emptiness of such a dream. The line that follows Blanca's declaration of what happiness is made of is undercut immediately by the women at work: "She plucked away at the turkeys, smiling to herself, as around her the older ladies sighed and shook their heads" (18). The women in Blanca's work area realize how fleeting the described happiness actually is. These women, unwilling to articulate to Blanca their own disillusionment, can only sigh and shake their heads at the entrapment Blanca is facing in this barrio community.

A succinctly articulated critique of patriarchy is not included in this narrative because Ponce's style is, to some extent, naturalistic. The characters she creates are swept along by events and forces outside their control. Society and "human nature" control a character's experience. Yet the narrator, by her ironic distance from her character, makes clear the limitations of a life in which a "wedding" is the highest form of happiness.

The Wedding attacks prescribed gender roles but offers no alternatives to its characters. As Anzaldúa suggests, it is only when we step beyond mere critique that an alternative or the beginnings of an alternative can be offered:

> But it is not enough to stand on the opposite river bank, shouting questions, challenging patriarchal, white conventions. . . . Because the counterstance stems from a problem with authority—outer as well as inner— it's a step towards liberation from cultural domination. But it is not a way of life. At some point, on our way to a new consciousness, we will have to leave the opposite bank, the split between the two mortal combatants somehow healed so that we are on both shores at once and, at once, see through serpent and eagle eyes. (Anzaldúa 78-79)

III. The Feminist Phase

Showalter's final phase, which I have renamed the feminist phase, extends "the feminist analysis of culture" by rejecting "both imitation and protest" (or, assimilation or accommodation) of male culture and moves to the articulation of female experience. It posits a historically informed analysis of patriarchy with a critique of that analysis in order to arrive at a new and autonomous self-identification. Gloria Anzaldúa identifies the identity of this new autonomous self as "the new Mestiza":

> . . . [L]*a mestiza* is a product of the transfer of the cultural and spiritual values of one group to another. . . . Cradled in one culture, sandwiched between two cultures, straddling all three cultures and their value systems, *la mestiza* undergoes a struggle of flesh, a struggle of borders, an inner war. . . .
>
> The new *mestiza* copes by developing a tolerance for contradictions, a tolerance for ambiguity. She learns to be an Indian in Mexican culture, to be Mexican from an Anglo point of view. She learns to juggle cultures. She has a plural personality, she operates in a pluralistic mode—nothing is thrust out, the good the bad and the ugly, nothing rejected, nothing abandoned. . . . It is where the possibility of uniting all that is separate occurs. This assembly is not one where severed or separated pieces merely come together. Nor is it a balancing of opposing powers. In attempting to work out a synthesis, the self has added a third element which is greater than the sum of its severed parts. That third element is a new consciousness—a mestiza consciousness—. . . . [I]ts energy comes from continual creative motion that keeps breaking down the unitary aspect of each new paradigm. (78-80)

The new mestiza is an identity informed by multiple histories (European, Latin American, indigenous, and United States), critical of those histories, yet realizing that the basis of the individual psyche is molded by these cultural experiences. Anzaldúa projects a new birth, a woman created from an identifiable past she is attempting to transcend. This new Mestiza chooses from the past, not necessarily discarding it but redefining those aspects of it that have marginalized women and "minorities."[1]

The conception is utopian and revisionist. This is a revolutionary and not merely a rebellious stance, represented most effectively by the conflicted woman character, a character attempting to balance contradictory social values, who recognizes the limitations of gender roles, sometimes offering an alternative to those roles. Attempting to articulate female experiences and resistance to patriarchy, authors who create characters caught in gender and "cultural collision" (78), as Anzaldúa calls it, are attempting to balance the ethnic and dominant cultures' demands (or as Anzaldúa adds, the demands of three cultures: United States, Mexican tradition, and the indigenous world) and definitions for appropriate gender roles.

The feminist phase in the work of contemporary Chicana writers is best identified by the demand for and recognition of subjectivity. The "I," in all its ambivalence, is voiced and heard and no longer muted; the female self begins actively to refuse the status of *object*. Cherríe Moraga, in the final pages of *Loving in the War Years*, voices the emergence of Chicana feminism:

> As a Chicana lesbian, I write of the connection my own feminism has had with my desire for women. *This is my story.* I can tell no other one than the one I understand. I eagerly await the writings by heterosexual Chicana feminists that can speak of their sexual desire for men and the ways in which their feminism informs that desire. (Emphasis mine 139)

The insistence on being heard, on being able to tell your own story, signals the beginnings of a feminist phase. *Trini* and *The Wedding* are told in third-person; the characters are the objects of the narrative. *Across the Great River* is in the first-person, but the self is constantly subservient to the authority of patriarchy. The first-person narratives in Chicana writings are the beginning of representing subjectivity, of telling "my story."

Yvonne Yarbro-Bejarano in "Chicana Literature From a Chicana Feminist Perspective" (1988) also comments upon the importance of subjectivity and taking a proprietary position in literature:

> The Chicana-identified critic also focuses on texts by Chicanas that involve a dual process of self-definition and building community with other Chicanas. In these works, *Chicanas are the subjects* of the representations, and often relationships between women form their crucial axes. . . . The process of self-definition involves what Black critic Bell Hooks calls moving from the margin to the center. White male writers take for granted the assumption of the subjective role to explore and understand self. The fact that Chicanas may tell stories about themselves and other Chicanas challenges the dominant male concepts of cultural ownership and literary authority. In telling these stories, Chicanas reject the dominant culture's definition of what a Chicana is. In writing, they refuse the objectification imposed by gender roles and racial and economic exploitation. (Emphasis mine 141)

Yarbro-Bejarano and Anzaldúa write the same story—the Chicana writer "learns to transform the small 'I' into the total Self" (Anzaldúa 83).

The novels of Cisneros, Castillo, Fernández and Chávez

exemplify this feminist voice. Their novels are in nontraditional forms and contribute to the development of the subjective feminist voice. The novels of Cisneros, Fernández, and Chávez are short stories loosely connected by the first-person narrative of their main characters. Castillo's novel, as Yarbro-Bejarano states, experiments with the epistolary form: "Ana Castillo plays with the conventions of the epistolary novel, undermining those conventions by inviting the reader to combine and recombine the individual letters in Cortazar fashion"(144). Experimenting with traditional forms and creating new ones, Chicana novelists realize the limitations of the old novelistic techniques in their search for their own voice. Eliana Ortega and Nancy Saporta Sternback in "At the Threshold of the Unnamed: Latina Literary Discourse in the Eighties," explain the new genres Latina writers are creating:

> Latina writers have not only occupied a new literary space, they have also created new genres. The majority of Latina literature has tended to be poetry, but recently they have developed a genre of their own, still to be defined and still emerging, which specifically articulates Latina experience. It draws on the Latina as a storyteller and situates the speaking voice in a genre somewhere in between poetry and fiction, blurring the line between the short story and the novel, between conversation and literary discourse. (17)

They cite the novels by Cisneros and Chávez as examples of this new genre; the description is especially true for Cisneros who admits that many of the stories in *Mango Street* are unfinished poems (Olivares 161). Ellen McCracken in "Sandra Cisneros' *The House on Mango Street*: Community-Oriented Introspection and the Demystification of Patriarchal Violence" (1989) states: "I prefer to classify Cisneros' text as a collection, a hybrid genre midway between the novel and the short story" (64).[2] Fernández' *Intaglio* has as its subtitle, *A Novel in Six Stories*. One would assume a contradiction, but the text is a coherent whole, a "collection" as Olivares calls them. Whatever the critics choose to call the genre, it is part of the new feminist Chicana consciousness.

Cisneros' novel has been one of the few nonpoetic works by a Chicana writer to receive wide critical attention. The development of a feminist identity is evident in *Mango Street*. In the fourth story, "My Name," Esperanza introduces herself: "In English my name means hope. In Spanish it means too many letters" (10). She explains whom she was named after:

> My great-grandmother. I would've liked to have known her, a wild horse of
> a woman, so wild she wouldn't marry until my great-grandfather threw a sack
> over her head and carried her off. Just like that, as if she were a fancy
> chandelier. That's the way he did it.
>
> And the story goes she never forgave him. She looked out the window
> all her life, the way so many women sit their sadness on an elbow. I wonder
> if she made the best with what she got or was she sorry because she couldn't
> be all the things she wanted to be. Esperanza. I have inherited her name, but
> I don't want to inherit her place by the window. (10-11)

irony

As Julián Olivares in "Sandra Cisneros' *The House on Mango Street*,
and the Poetics of Space" (1988) claims: "In this vignette Esperanza
traces the reason for the discomfiture with her name to cultural
oppression, the Mexican males' suppression of their women" (163).
Realizing the status of women in the culture, Esperanza "prefers a
name not culturally embedded in a dominating, male-centered
ideology" (163). She would like to become someone and not inherit
the place her great-grandmother was forced to accept. In order to
escape the cultural baggage of patriarchy, Esperanza would like to
name herself, create her own identity:

> I would like to baptize myself under a new name, a name more like the real
> me, the one nobody sees. Esperanza as Lisandra or Maritza or Zeze the X. Yes.
> Something like Zeze the X will do. (11)

By baptizing herself, Esperanza can cleanse herself of the past and
begin anew without a predestined role in patriarchy.

Cisneros says, in an interview with Pilar E. Rodríguez Aranda
(1990), that this novel is not autobiographical but "true":

> What I'm doing is I'm writing true stories. They're all stories I lived, or
> witnessed, or heard; stories that were told to me. I collected those stories and
> I arranged them in an order so they would be clear and cohesive. Because in
> real life, there's no order. (64)[3]

True!

The stories are of those people Cisneros grew up with and especially
of the women who lived in the barrio and influenced Esperanza:
". . . it is the fate of the women in her *barrio* that has the most
profound impact on her, especially as she begins to develop sexually

and learns that the same fate might be hers" (Yarbro-Bejarano 142).
In the story "Marin," Esperanza tells us that Marin is from Puerto Rico,
is fun, she gossips and talks endlessly about boys and boyfriends:
"What matters, Marin says, is for the boys to see us and for us to see
them" (27). Esperanza, however, seems to understand the limitations
of living just for male attention: "Marin, under the streetlight,
dancing by herself, is singing the same song somewhere. I know. Is
waiting for a car to stop, a star to fall, someone to change her life"
(27). The image emphasizes the loneliness and passivity in feminine
self-objectification.

　　Like Marin, Rosa Vargas is trapped within conventional
femininity. This woman's existence is defined by so many children
that she cannot control them. Esperanza is quick to point out that it
is not Rosa Vargas' fault for all the trouble but the failure of the absent
male:

> Rosa Vargas' kids are too many and too much. It's not her fault you
> know, except she is their mother and only one against so many.
> 　　They are bad those Vargas, and how can they help it with only one
> mother who is tired all the time from buttoning and bottling and babying, and
> who cries every day for the man who left without even leaving a dollar for
> bologna or a note explaining how come. (29)

This sort of unexplained but common victimization of women also
includes "patriarchal violence in its more overt stages" (McCracken
67): child abuse, wife abuse, and rape. Esperanza is raped in the story
"Red Clowns": "Sally, you lied. It wasn't what you said at all. What
he did. Where he touched me. I didn't want it, Sally. The way they
said it, the way it's supposed to be, all the storybooks and movies,
why did you lie to me?"(99). María Herrera-Sobek in "The Politics of
Rape: Sexual Transgression in Chicana Fiction" (1988) sees this story
as a strong indictment of "the perpetrators of the sex-is-glamorous
myth" (178). For Esperanza, "They all lied. All the books and
magazines, everything that told it wrong" (Cisneros 100). Esperanza
realizes that it could be her fate to be trapped in the misogyny of the
barrio as are so many of the women of her community. And a key
difference between this text and those in the "feminine" or "female"
traditions is a stronger focus on Mexican-American sexism in the
barrio, than on racism and poverty. This does not necessarily imply
a negation of racism or poverty as problems, but the feminist sees

gender at the center of the matrix of race and class.

Esperanza's escape "is linked in the text to education and above all her writing" (Yarbro-Bejarano 143). It is the second aspect, the idea of authorship, of empowering the self by telling her own story that characterizes Esperanza's response as feminist:

> I like to tell stories. I tell them inside my head. I tell them after the mailman says here's your mail. . . .
> I make a story for my life, for each step my brown shoe takes. (109)

The appropriateness of the "I," the acknowledgement that Esperanza can voice her own story makes her able "to say goodbye to Mango," but with the promise to return and help others. For Cisneros, included in the responsibility to self is the responsibility to the community: "They will not know I have gone away to come back. For the ones I left behind" (102). Yarbro-Bejarano accurately emphasizes the relationship between the "I" and the community:

> *The House on Mango St.* captures the dialectic between self and community in Chicana writing. Esperanza finds her literary voice through her own cultural experience and that of other Chicanas. She seeks self-empowerment through writing, while recognizing her commitment to a community of Chicanas. Writing has been essential in connecting her with the power of women . . . . (143)

Finding power in writing and asserting the subjective "I" while simultaneously connecting to and empowering the community is central to the feminist phase and a similar theme in Ana Castillo's *The Mixquiahuala Letters* (1986). Here the "dialectic between self and community" centers on the formal relationship in the epistolary novel among writer, reader, and letter writers. Yarbro-Bejarano notes the importance of "exchange" in this form:

> The novel defines subjectivity in relation to another woman, and the bond between the two women further cemented by the epistolary examination of their relationship is as important as the exploration of self through writing. (144)

The subjectivity defined by the relationship between Teresa and Alicia is the essence of this novel. This is further illustrated by Teresa's insistence upon a lower-case "i" and a possible allusion to the Spanish term *yo* which represents the subjective "I" and is always lower cased. This is a shared "i"; it belongs to both Teresa who writes the letters and Alicia who receives them. In the letters, Teresa writes of her own and Alicia's life. We never see a letter from Alicia. Teresa, however, is able to provide the stories of each woman because of her faith in their shared experience and identity: "i know what you're thinking, Alicia . . ."; "you scrutinized me with artist's eyes . . ."; "you enjoyed telling . . ."; "you told me . . ."; "you . . . you . . . you thought . . . " (47, 58, 131). The use of "you" throughout the letters brings the reader into Alicia's life as well.

But Teresa employs the third person on herself when she is experiencing herself as object, rather than subject, especially when describing the intense and difficult relationships she has with men:

> Until i succeed in boring him with my persistence to remind him of commitments, *that*, at least kept his interest. . . .
> She may have a clue that he has found someone else to capture his interest. She now looks like the shadow of the new woman who radiates with his passionate attention. (112)

Too threatening for Teresa's subjective self, she distances the situation by writing about herself in the third person. The volatile relationships between men and women cause Teresa to acknowledge the personal damage to herself and her understanding of how Alicia could hate herself:

> You weren't the desirable, soft, uncomplicated, maternal/child, buxom, ever-enduring lap and embrace, blonde, vivacious, cherry red puckered-lipped, plastic starlet of Hollywood movies, the saintly madonna, any image, illusion, delusion, hallucination, glossy, celluloid reproduction, stereotype, cliched man's definition of what a woman is and has to be. Therefore, you would not be *loved*. (113)

For Teresa and Alicia, the battle ground upon which heterosexual women collide defines their relationship with men: the Hollywood-enforced Anglo patriarchal expectations for women, which Teresa and Alicia are trying to escape.

Teresa's marriage to Libra is described as the tensions between a man and "his" woman. Admitting that Libra will listen to men before he notices his wife, Teresa realizes that she must leave him:

i may have been Libra's wife with considerable influence but Melvin was a man and a man's woman could not compete with that. . . . i packed my duffle bag with jeans, books, and poems and moved out on my own. (35)

Alicia has similar difficulties with men, and Norma Alarcón (1989) succinctly comprehends the crux of the matter:

The patriarchal promise of romantic/erotic bliss, *re*-presented in all manner of popular literature, is an ideological maneuver to kill their subjectivity and any further exploration of their own desire. (104)

Both Teresa and Alicia gradually understand this concept and find in their correspondence, in the act of communicating, the ability to assert the subjective and find nurturance: "We were experts at exchanging empathy for heart-rending confusion known only to lovers, but you and i had never been lovers" (121). Teresa goes on to say they were "closer" than lovers, "a single entity, nondiscriminate of the other's being" (122). They fused together into the subjective lower-case "i," refusing the objectification of the other bound up in heterosexual norms.

The bonding between these women is a response to the patriarchal demands that attempt to submerge their subjectivity. Teresa offers a feminist vision for her own male child:

The following day at the airport, i gave you a list of general instructions if Vittorio should ever become yours: he should be taught to look after himself, mend his own clothes, cook, clean up and do his share. He should be allowed to do whatever it was that little boys liked to do but he should also be sensitive...

You smiled and gave me a peck on the cheek without looking into my eyes. i watched until you disappeared down the ramp. Next to you went a man you tried to teach all the things i had just told you Vittorio must learn if he was to grow up to be a decent companion to a woman. (130)

For Teresa and Alicia, the lack of a "decent companion" in men represents a loss and one that will continue until the feminist vision she describes becomes ingrained in their society. In this scene, Alicia walks off with a man who will kill himself as an act of revenge upon her. Clearly, the "new consciousness" has not yet been achieved. But in the strength of the relationship between Alicia and Teresa one finds the feminist alternative to the oppression of patriarchy. The ability to tell their story, the lower-case "i" representing both, articulates the subjectivity that would otherwise be stripped from them.

Denise Chávez in *The Last of the Menu Girls* also creates a character whose insistence upon her own subjectivity represents a feminist alternative. The willingness to "look back" (Alarcón 1988, 150) in order to construct an identity from the past is common in the works of Cisneros, Castillo, Chávez, and Fernández. Chávez begins her novel with Rocío being identified by an official job application form:

> NAME: Rocío Esquibel
> AGE: Seventeen
> PREVIOUS EXPERIENCE WITH THE SICK AND DYING: My Great Aunt Eutilia
> PRESENT EMPLOYMENT: Work-study aide at Altavista Memorial   (13)

This is Rocío officially, but it is not she. The rest of the novel is dedicated to Rocío's search for an identity: "I want to be someone else, somewhere else, someone important and responsible and sexy" (34). The stories, like those in Cisneros' novel, are loosely connected but cumulative. In "Shooting Stars," Rocío wonders about becoming a woman:

> What did it mean to be a woman? To be beautiful, complete? Was beauty a physical or a spiritual thing, was it strength of emotion, resolve, a willingness to love? What was it then, that made women lovely? (53)

The ability to write one's own story and her community's stories is "what [makes] women lovely" and Chávez echoes Cisneros' own connection between individual subjectivity and the community: "'Rocío, just write about this little street of ours, it's only one block long, but there's so many stories'" (190). As Chávez states in "Heat and Rain (Testimonio)" (1989), "I write about what I know, who I am" (32). By asserting a Chicana subjectivity, the phallocentrism and Eurocentrism are shifted. "Who I am" and "what I know" become legitimated in narrative form. While the patriarchy may still engulf existence, the assertion of the subjective by these authors provides another vision, a feminist one.

Notes

1 The term "minorities" to identify those groups who are not "Anglo" in United States society is actually an inaccuracy. Throughout the world, Anglos are in the minority, and in the United States, as demographics continue to shift, Anglos will become the minority in the twenty-first century.

2 This "hybrid genre" can also classify other works like Sherwood Anderson's *Winesburg, Ohio*, William Faulkner's *Go Down, Moses*, and Gloria Naylor's *The Women of Brewster Place*.

3 Aranda's interview with Cisneros is entitled "On the Solitary Fate of Being Mexican, Female, Wicked and Thirty-three: An Interview with Writer Sandra Cisneros."

Fe (Faith) in American Dism
Esperanza (Hope) in the New
meztise

Conclusion

Toward an Indigenous Feminism

> As a *mestiza* I have no country, my homeland cast me out; yet all countries are mine because I am every woman's sister or potential lover. (As a lesbian I have no race, my own people disclaim me; but I am all races because there is the queer of me in all races.) I am cultureless because, as a feminist, I challenge the collective cultural/religious male-derived beliefs of Indo-Hispanics and Anglos; yet I am participating in the creation of yet another culture, a new story to explain the world and our participation in it, a new value system with images and symbols that connect us to each other and to the planet. *Soy un amasamiento*, I am an act of kneading, of uniting and joining that not only has produced both a creature of darkness and a creature of light, but also a creature that questions the definitions of light and dark and gives them new meanings. (Anzaldúa 80-81)[1]

The folk healer/medicine woman/spiritual healer/fortune teller/*bruja* (the witch)/herbal healer—all these terms represent the *curandera* in Chicano culture. A woman who inhabits Anzaldúa's borderland, a woman of the light and the dark, of good and evil, of Catholicism and indigenous rituals, but, above all, she is a woman who heals through the use of herbs and prayers. Like the medicine woman, Anzaldúa also tries to heal. For Anzaldúa, as writer, as new mestiza consciousness, as border inhabitant, her work "lies in healing the split that originates in the very foundation of our lives, our culture, our languages, our thoughts" (80). This image of the writer as curandera can represent the task Chicana feminist writers are trying to accomplish. In the same way these authors have recovered the image of La Malinche, retelling, revisioning, reappropriating from patriarchy's Malintzin, they also can rediscover the fortune teller/*la bruja*/the herbal healer. Accepting the complex/contradictory image of the *curandera* and refusing to allow the good and evil to be separated away from that image, the Chicana feminist writer can heal the splits of duality and encompass more of the cultural specific experience in their work.[2]

The work of the Chicana *curandera* feminist writer is defined by Anzaldúa as a process occurring in the borderland of the soul:

> It is where the possibility of uniting all that is separate occurs. This assembly is not one where severed or separated pieces merely come together. Nor is it a balancing of opposing powers. In attempting to work out a synthesis, the self has added a third element which is greater than the sum of its severed parts. That third element is a new consciousness—a mestiza consciousness—and though it is a source of intense pain, its energy comes from continual creative motion that keeps breaking down the unitary aspect of each new paradigm. (80)

To be able to encompass all, to disregard only after she has understood and found something wanting, to accept good and evil and reinterpret meanings: this represents the process of the new mestiza consciousness and the writers who want to include all Mexican-American women's experience. This new consciousness, however, is a developing one; it is a process without clear and obvious outcomes or even goals, merely visions of a less violent and destructive world. It is also what I call an indigenous feminism, a feminism that acknowledges the cultures, communities, and histories that have created this consciousness.

Writing is also a process, and the works of the Chicana novelists and critics in this study continue to be published. These authors are not turning their backs on the Chicana, or on articulating her experiences, exploring her conscience and consciousness. They have only begun the work of understanding multicultural experience, of finding a language for it, of clarifying the matrix of class, race, gender, sexual orientation, and other variables not yet imagined. The process, however, has begun, and it cannot be silenced now.

When I first began this project, in the spring of 1988, only five of the ten novels were published. Today, with publishing houses more willing to publish these authors, with new authors and books available, just maybe the Chicana/Latina/Hispanic/Mexican-American writer is following the literary steps of her African-American sisters and representing the acknowledged contemporary voices of American literature. The works of Toni Morrison, Alice Walker, Audre Lorde, Gloria Naylor, Paule Marshall, June Jordan, Jamaica Kincaid will be accompanied by the works of Gloria Anzaldúa, Ana Castillo, Denise Chávez, Sandra Cisneros, Mary Helen Ponce, Margarita Cota-Cárdenas,

Estela Portillo Trambley, Lucha Corpi, Irene Beltrán Hernández, Roberta Fernández, Laura del Fuego, Cherríe Moraga, and those who will publish after them.

I offer speculation, but I offer an assurance, this new voice will not disappear. Chicana novelists will write, for they have found an audience and an audience has found them. The silence of the past four hundred fifty years is being broken. A new written word is appearing; a once invisible, often despised, muted experience heard only in the oral tradition has found a more permanent form, the written word. It may still be a whisper in a crowded room, but it is growing in strength; it is moving into the center; it is different and the same and new and old and not any of those. I hear that voice. Come a little closer. I know you can hear it too. Listen as the voice of La Malinche/la mestiza/la curandera offers a prayer echoing another voice that started as a whisper.

Notes

1 Anzaldúa is echoing Virginia Woolf's *Three Guineas* (1936): "'For,' the outsider will say, 'in fact, as a woman, I have no country. As a woman I want no country. As a woman my country is the whole world'" (109).

2 I need to acknowledge Professor Patrick Mullen of Ohio State University for first pointing-out to me the connection between the writer and the image of the *curandera*.

Bibliography

Alarcón, Norma. "Chicana's Feminist Literature: A Re-vision Through Malintzin/or Malintzin: Putting Flesh back on the Object." Moraga, *This Bridge* 182–90.

———."Making 'Familia' From Scratch: Split Subjectivities in the Work of Helena Maria Viramontes and Cherríe Moraga." Herrera-Sobek, *Chicana Creativity* 147–59.

———."The Sardonic Powers of the Erotic in the Work of Ana Castillo." Horno-Delgado 94–107.

———."Interview with Cherríe Moraga." *Third Woman* (1986): 126–34.

Alcalá, Kathleen J. *Mrs. Vargas and the Dead Naturalist*. Corvalis, OR: Calyx Books, 1992.

Anzaldúa, Gloria. *Borderlands/La Frontera: The New Mestiza*. San Francisco: Spinsters/Aunt Lute, 1987.

———, ed. *Making Face, Making Soul, Haciendo Caras: Creative and Critical Perspectives by Women of Color*. San Francisco: Aunt Lute, 1990.

——— and Cherríe Moraga, eds. *This Bridge Called My Back*.

Barreca, Regina, ed. *Last Laughs: Perspectives on Women and Comedy*. New York: Gordon and Breach, 1988.

Beardsmore, Hugo Baetens. *Bilingualism: Basic Principles*. Clevedon, England: Multilingual Matters, 1986.

Beltrán Hernández, Irene. *Across the Great River*. Houston: Arte Público P, 1989.

———. *Heart Beat Drum Beat*. Houston: Arte Público P, 1992.

Benstock, Shari, ed. *Feminist Issues in Literary Scholarship*. Bloomington: Indiana U P, 1987.

Blea, Irene I. *La Chicana and the Intersection of Race, Class, and Gender*. New York: Praeger, 1992.

Boza, María del Carmen, et. al., eds. *Nosotros: Latina Literature Today*. Binghamton: Bilingual P, 1986.

Brown, Linda Keller and Kay Mussell, eds. *Ethnic and Regional Foodways in the United States: The Performance of Group Identity*. Knoxvilled: U of Tennessee P, 1984.

Castillo, Ana. *The Mixquiahuala Letters*. Binghamton: Bilingual P, 1986.

———. *Sapogonia*. Tempe, AZ: Bilingual P, 1990.

———. *So Far From God*. New York: Norton, 1993.

Chapman, Raymond. "The reader as listener: dialect and relationships in *The Mayor of Casterbridge*." *The Pragmatics of Style*. Ed. L. Hickey. London: Routledge 1989. 159-78.

Chávez, Denise. *The Last of the Menu Girls*. Houston: Arte Publico P, 1986.

———. *Face of an Angel*. New York: Farrar, Straus and Giroux, 1994.

———. "Heat and Rain (testimonio)." Horno-Delgado 27-32.

Cisneros, Sandra. *The House on Mango Street*. New York: Vintage, 1989.

_____. *Woman Hollering Creek and Other Stories*. New York: Random House, 1991.

Cixous, Hélène. "The Laugh of the Medusa." Marks 245-64.

Córdova, Teresa, Norma Cantú, Gilberto Cardenas, Juan García, and Christine M. Sierra. *Chicana Voices: Intersections of Class, Race, and Gender*. Albuquerque: U New Mexico P and NACS, 1990.

Corpi, Lucha. *Delia's Song*. Houston: Arte Público P, 1989.

_____. *Eulogy to a Brown Angel: A Mystery Novel*. Houston: Arte Público P, 1992.

Cortés, Carlos E., ed. *Church Views of the Mexican American*. New York: Arno, 1974.

Cota-Cárdenas, Margarita. *Puppet*. Austin: Relámpago Books P, 1985.

Cotera, Marta. "Feminism: The Chicana and the Anglo versions, a historical analysis." Melville 217-34.

Cypress, Sandra Messinger. *La Malinche in Mexican Literature: From History to Myth*. Austin: U of Texas P, 1991.

Dasenbrock, Reed Way. "Intelligibility and Meaningfulness in Multicultural Literature in English." *PMLA*. 102.1 (1987): 10-19.

de Dwyer, Carlota Cárdenas, ed. *Chicano Voices*. Boston: Houghton, 1975.

De Leon, Arnoldo. *Ethnicity in the Sunbelt: A History of Mexican Americans in Houston*. Houston: Mexican American Studies at U Houston, 1989.

de Valdez, Theresa A. "Organizing as a Political Tool for the Chicana." *Frontiers*. 5.2 (1980): 7-13.

Del Castillo, Adelaida R. "Malintzin Tenépal: A Preliminary Look into a New Perspective." Sánchez, *La Mujer* 124-49.

del Fuego, Laura. *Maravilla*. Encino: Floricanto P, 1989.

Dewey, Janice. "Dona Josefa: Bloodpulse of Transition and Change." Horno-Delgado 39-47.

Eliot, George. *Middlemarch*. Boston: Houghton, 1956.

Esperanza. "Siembra." *National Latina Health Organization Bilingual Newsletter*. 1.1 (1990-1991): 6-7.

Fernández, Roberta. *Intaglio: A Novel in Six Stories*. Houston: Arte Público P, 1990.

____, ed. *In Other Words: Literature by Latinas of the United States*. Houston: Arte Publico P, 1994.

Fisher, Dexter, ed. *The Third Women: Minority Women Writers of the United States*. Boston: Houghton, 1980.

Furman, Nelly. "The Politics of Language: Beyond the Gender Principle?" Greene 59-79.

Gómez, Alma, Cherríe Moraga, and Mariana Romo-Carmona, eds. *Cuentos: Stories by Latinas*. New York: Kitchen Table/Women of Color P, 1983.

Gonzales-Berry, Erlinda. *Paletitos de guayaba*. Albuquerque: Academia/El Norte P, 1991

Gonzales, Sylvia. "The White Feminist Movement: The Chicana Perspective." *Social Science Journal* 14 (1977): 67-76.

Greene, Gayle and Coppelia Kahn, eds. *Making a Difference: Feminist Literary Criticism*. New York: Methuen, 1985.

_____. "Feminist Scholarship and the Social Construction of Woman." Greene 1-36.

Hajuta, Kenji. *Mirror of Language: The Debate on Bilingualism*. New York: Basic Books, 1986.

Herrera-Sobek, María, ed. *Beyond Stereotypes: The Critical Analysis of Chicana Literature*. Binghamton: Bilingual P, 1985.

_____.and Helena María Viramontes, ed. *Chicana Creativity and Criticism: Charting New Frontiers in American Literature*. Houston: Arte Público P, 1988.

_____*The Mexican Corrido: A Feminist Analysis*. Bloomington: Indiana U P, 1990.

_____. "The Politics of Rape: Sexual Transgression in Chicana Fiction." Herrera-Sobek, *Chicana Creativity* 171-81.

_____, ed. *Reconstructing a Chicano/a Literary Heritage: Hispanic Colonial Literature of the Southwest*. Tucson: U Arizona P, 1993.

Horno-Delgado, Asunción, et al., eds. *Breaking Boundaries: Latina Writings and Critical Readings*. Amherst: U of Massachusetts P, 1989.

Hull, Gloria T. *Reading Literature by U.S. Third World Women*. Wellesley: Wellesley College, Center for Research on Women, Working Paper no. 141, 1984.

_____, Patricia Bell Scott, and Barbara Smith, eds. *All the Women Are White, All the Blacks Are Men, But Some of Us Are Brave: Black Women's Studies*. New York: Feminist P, 1982.

Irigaray, Luce. *Speculum of the Other Woman*. Trans. Gillian C. Gill. Ithaca: Cornell U P, 1985.

_____. *This Sex Which Is Not One*. Trans. Catherine Porter. Ithaca: Cornell U P, 1985.

Kanellos, Nicolás, ed. *The Hispanic-American Almanac: A Reference Work on Hispanics in the United States*. Detroit: Gale, 1993.

Kaplan, Carey and Ellen Cronan Rose. *The Canon and the Common Reader*. Knoxville: U of Tennessee P, 1990.

Kloss, Heinz. *The American Bilingual Tradition*. Rowley: Newbury, 1977.

Lomelí, Francisco A. "Chicana Novelists in the Process of Creating Fictive Voices." Herrera-Sobek, *Beyond Stereotypes* 29-46.

López, Arcadia. *Barrio Teacher*. Houston: Arte Publico P, 1992.

Lucero, Marcela C. "Resources for the Chicana Feminist Scholar." Treichler 393-401.

Lucero-Trujillo, Marcela Christine. "The Dilemma of the Modern Chicana Artist and Critic." Fisher 324-32.

Luna Lawhn, Juanita, et al. eds. *Mexico and the United States: Intercultural Relations in the Humanities*. San Antonio: San Antonio College/The Mexican Cultural Institute, 1984.

McCracken, Ellen. "Sandra Cisneros' *The House on Mango Street*: Community-Oriented Introspection and the Demystification of Patriarchal Violence." Horno-Delgado 62-71.

McKay, Sandra L. and Sau-ling Cynthia Wong, eds. *Languag and Diversity: Problem or Resource?* Cambridge: Newbury House, 1988.

McKenna, Teresa and Flora Ida Ortiz, eds. *The Broken Web: The Educational Experience of Hispanic American Women*. Encino: Floricanto P and The Tomás Rivera Center, 1988.

Macklin, June. "'All the good and bad in this world': Women, traditional medicine, and Mexican American culture." Melville 127-48.

Marcus, Jane. "Daughters of Anger/Material Girls: Con/Textualizing Feminist Criticism." Barreca 281-308.

Marks, Elaine and Isabelle de Courtivron, eds. *New French Feminisms: An Anthology.* New York: Schocken, 1981.

Martínez, Eliud. "Personal Vision in the Short Stories of Estela Portillo Trambley." Herrera-Sobek, *Beyond Stereotypes* 71-90.

Mendheim, Beverly. *Ritchie Valens: The First Latino Rocker.* Tempe, AZ: Bilingual P, 1987.

Melville, Margarita B., ed. *Twice a Minority: Mexican American Women.* St. Louis: Mosby, 1980.

Miller, Beth, ed. *Women in Hispanic Literature: Icons and Fallen Idols.* Berkeley: U of California P, 1984.

Mirandí, Alfredo and Evangelina Enríquez. *La Chicana: The Mexican American Woman.* Chicago: U of Chicago P, 1979.

Modin, Sandra. "The Depiction of the Chicana in *Bless Me, Ultima* and *The Milagro Beanfield War*: A Study in Contrasts." Luna Lawhn, 137-150.

Moi, Toril. *Sexual/Textual Politics: Feminist Literary Criticism.* New York: Methuen, 1985.

Mora, Magdalena and Adelaida R. del Castillo, eds. *Mexican Women in the United States: Struggles Past and Present.* Los Angeles: Chicano Studies Center and U of California, 1980.

Moraga, Cherríe. *Loving in the War Years: lo que nunca pasó por sus labios.* Boston: South End P, 1983.

_____ and Gloria Anzaldúa, eds. *This Bridge Called My Back: Writings by Radical Women of Color*. New York: Kitchen Table/ Women of Color Press, 1983.

Munich, Adrienne. "Notorious Signs, Feminist Criticism and Literary Tradition." Greene 238-59.

Murguía, Edward. *Chicano Intermarriage: A Theoretical and Empirical Study*. San Antonio: Trinity U P, 1982.

Ordoñez, Elizabeth J. "The Concept of Cultural Identity in Chicana Poetry." *Third Woman* 2.1 (1984): 75-82.

_____. "Sexual Politics and the Theme of Sexuality in Chicana Poetry." Miller 316-39.

Olivares, Julián. "Sandra Cisneros' *The House on Mango Street* and the Poetics of Space." Herrera-Sobek, *Chicana Creativity* 160-70.

Ornelas, Berta. *Come Down from the Mound*. Phoenix: Miter P, 1975.

Ortega, Eliana and Nancy Saporta Sternback. "At the Threshold of the Unnamed: Latina Literary Discourse in the Eighties." Horno-Delgado 2-23.

Ortiz Taylor, Sheila. *Faultline*. Tallahassee: Naiad P, 1982.

_____. *Spring Forward/Fall Back*. Tallahassee: Naiad P, 1985.

_____. *Slow Dancing at Miss Molly's*. Tallahassee: Naiad P, 1989.

_____. *Southbound*. Tallahassee: Naiad P, 1990.

Paz, Octavio. *The Labyrinth of Solitude, Life and Thought in Mexico*. Trans. Lysander Kemp. New York: Grove, 1961.

Pérez-Erdélyi, Mireya. "Entrevista con Lucha Corpi: Poeta Chicana." *The Americas Review* 17.1 (1989): 72-82.

Phillips, Rachel. "Marina/Malinche: Masks and Shadows." Miller 97-114.

Ponce, Mary Helen. *Taking Control*. Houston: Arte Público P, 1987.

———. *The Wedding*. Houston: Arte Público P, 1989.

Portillo Trambley, Estela. *Trini*. Binghamton: Bilingual P, 1986.

———. *Rain of Scorpions and Other Writings*. Berkeley: Tonatiuh, 1975.

Ramirez, Arthur. Rev. of *Borderlands/La Frontera* by Gloria Anzaldúa. *The Americas Review* 17.3-4 (1989): 185-87.

Ramos, Juanita, ed. *Compañeras: Latina Lesbians (An Anthology)*. New York: Latina Lesbian History Project, 1987.

Rebolledo, Tey Diana. "Game Theory in Chicana Poetry." Vigil 159-68.

———. "The Politics of Poetics: Or, What Am I, A Critic, Doing in This Text Anyhow?" Herrera-Sobek, *Chicana Creativity* 129-38.

———. "Walking the Thin Line: Humor in Chicana Literature." Herrera-Sobek, *Beyond Stereotypes* 91-107.

——— and Eliana S. Rivero, eds. *Infinite Divisions: An Anthology of Chicana Literature*. Tucson: U Arizona P, 1993.

Redfern, Bernice. *Women of Color in the United States: A Guide to the Literature*. New York: Garland, 1989.

Ríos, Isabella. *Victuum*. Ventura, CA: Diana-Etna, 1976.

Rodríguez, Andrés and Roberto G. Trujillo, eds. *Literatura Chicana, Creative and Critical Writings Through 1984*. Encino: Floricanto P, 1985.

Rodríguez Aranda, Pilar E. "On the Solitary Fate of Being Mexican, Female, Wicked and Thirty-three: An Interview with Writer Sandra Cisneros." *The Americas Review* 18.1 (1990): 64–80.

Salazar Parr, Carmen and Genevieve M. Ramírez. "The Female Heroin Chicano Literature." Herrera-Sobek, *Beyond Stereotypes* 47-60.

Sánchez, Marta. *Contemporary Chicana Poetry: A Critical Approach to an Emerging Literature*. Berkeley: U of California P, 1984.

Sánchez, Rosaura. "Chicana Prose Writers: The Case of Gina Valdés and Sylvia Lizárraga." Herrera-Sobek, *Beyond Stereotypes* 61-70.

_____ and Rosa Martinez Cruz, eds. *Essays on La Mujer*. Los Angeles: Chicano Studies Center, U of California, 1977.

_____. *Chicano Discourse: Socio-Historic Perspectives*. Rowley: Newbury House, 1983.

Silva, Beverly. *The Cat and Other Stories*. Tempe: Bilingual P, 1986.

Showalter, Elaine, ed. *The New Feminist Criticism: Essays on Women, Literature and Theory*. New York: Pantheon, 1985.

_____. "The Feminist Critical Revolution." Showalter, *New Feminist Criticism* 3-17.

_____. "Toward a Feminist Poetics." Showalter, *New Feminist Criticism* 125-43.

_____. "Feminist Criticism in the Wilderness." Showalter, *New Feminist Criticism* 243-70.

_____. "Women's Time, Women's Space: Writing the History of Feminist Criticism." Benstock 30-44.

Sternback, Nancy Saporta. "'A Deep Racial Memory of Love': The Chicana Feminism of Cherríe Moraga." Horno-Delgado 48-61.

Tatum, Charles M. *The New Chicana/Chicano Writing*. Tucson: U of Arizona P, 1992.

Tharp, Roland G., et al. "Changes in Marriage Roles Accompanying the Acculturation of a Mexican-American Wife." *Journal of Marriage and Family* 30 (1986): 404-12.

Treichler, Paula A., Cheris Kramarae, and Beth Stafford, eds. *For Alma Mater: Theory and Practice in Feminist Scholarship*. Urbana: U of Illinois P, 1985.

Trujillo, Carla, ed. *Chicana Lesbians: The Girls Our Mothers Warned Us About*. Berkeley: Third Woman P, 1991.

Valdés, Gina. *There Are No Madmen Here*. San Diego: Maize P, 1981.

Valdés, Guadalupe. "The Language Situation of Mexican Americans." McKay 111-39.

Vélez, Diana, ed. *Reclaiming Medusa: Short Stories by Contemporary Puerto Rican Women*. San Francisco: Spinsters/Aunt Lute, 1988.

Vigil, Evangelina, ed. *Woman of Her Word: Hispanic Women Write*. Houston: Arte Público P, 1987.

Villanueva, Alma Luz. *The Ultraviolet Sky*. Tempe, AZ: Bilingual P, 1988.

_____. *Naked Ladies*. Tempe, AZ: Bilingual P, 1994.

_____. *Weeping Woman: La Llorona and Other Stories*. Tempe, AZ: Blingual P, 1994.

Viramontes, Helena María. *The Moths and Other Stories*. Houston: Arte Público P, 1985.

Williams, Brett. "Why Migrant Women Feed Their Husbands Tamales: Foodways as a Basis for a Revisionist View of Tejano Family Life." Brown 113-26.

Votaw, Carmen D. "Cultural Influences on Hispanic Feminism." *Agenda* 11.4 (1981): 44-49.

Woolf, Virginia. *Three Guineas*. New York: Harcourt, 1966.

Yarbro-Bejarano, Yvonne. "Chicana Literature from a Chicana Feminist Perspective." Herrera-Sobek, *Chicana Creativity* 139-46.

Zamora, Emilio. *The World of the Mexican Worker in Texas*. College Station: Texas A&M U P, 1993.

Index